TOAD IN MY GARDEN

RUCHIRA MUKERJEE was born and brought up in
the northern province of Uttar Pradesh and was educated
mainly in Lucknow and Allahabad. She lives in Bombay
where she works in the Department of Telecommunications. She is a practising Buddhist. *Toad in My Garden* is
her first novel.

Ruchira Mukerjee

TOAD IN MY GARDEN

PICADOR

First published 1998 by Picador

This edition published 1999 by Picador
an imprint of Macmillan Publishers Ltd
25 Eccleston Place, London SW1W 9NF
and Basingstoke

Associated companies throughout the world

ISBN 0 330 36951 2

A CIP catalogue record for this book is available from
the British Library.

Typeset by SetSystems Ltd, Saffron Walden, Essex
Printed and bound in Great Britain by
Mackays of Chatham plc, Chatham, Kent

Dedicated to Sensei, Daisaku Ikeda

ACKNOWLEDGEMENTS

I express my grateful thanks to Mr Ravi Dayal for his suggestions, and to my friends Rajaram and Ramchandran, without whom this book would not have been possible. My special thanks to my mother, my sister Mondira, my friend Komi Raote, and to Varsha Das for their daimoku, concern and wise counsel. My deep gratitude also to Pankaj Mishra who made the important things happen.

CHAPTER ONE

Others have heard this story before, the parts I chose to tell, about my attraction to an older man, love letters, and the magical spoken words we exchanged in those days. But they heard it when events still lacked coherence; and they found the tale romantic, moving, even outrageous. I am retelling it today to insinuate into those random-seeming events some kind of significance — so that others can recognize that the romance was not the story but a young woman's craving for intensity beyond intelligent survival, her fear of dullness and comfort; her predisposition to a certain kind of life.

More simply, it began one July evening in Allahabad when I was twelve years old. My father, Biren, and I were out visiting his uncle, Sachi-mama, who had a thirteen-year-old daughter I was friends with. Bela and I huddled continually in corners to exchange the urgent, unsavoury secrets of our age, body hair and who had got her period recently. Actually, when they happened to us, we both rather hated the business of menstruation and brassières, the curious measuring gaze of adults who had had no time for us before. On the other hand, there was that horrid, transfixing quality to abdominal pain, the recurrent darkening emissions and trussings-up that constituted adolescence, which having caught our imagination once, held it for years afterwards. On that evening, half-dead with the heat, we played checkers and then lay at last with our cheeks to the cool floor, examining with dim longing photographs of a film star, Uttam Kumar.

Suddenly, Bela rolled over and vanished under a huge four-poster. I followed her and, in an instant, my nose met up with six pairs of gleaming shoes, rust, a patterned brown, dandy off-white and a muted black among them. That's my brother, said Bela, he's home on annual leave. (So there was a brother, stylish, adventurous, a captain with the armoured corps.) Bela, whom I had met just six months ago when we moved to Allahabad, acquired a new interest in my eyes. The sambar skin nudged the suede in a gentle excitement and he gained flesh before my eyes as Bela and I, still under the four-poster, leafed through a hidden photograph album. Captain Haldar at a beauty contest, standing between four dewy, laughing girls in swimsuits, then pictures of the new-found relative in an embroidered, high-collar dinner jacket (DJ, Bela called it) and cummerbund, or sitting atop a tank.

'I must leave now. Where are the girls?' called my father suddenly, standing beside the big bed. 'Megha's come without telling her mother.'

We emerged then, rumpled, dusty, grinning, our dreams of glamour tucked hastily away behind the startled, nudging shoes. There were two pairs with spurs on them, something I had never seen before.

I was soon out in the ripe, bursting warmth of the evening with Biren who was starting up his blue-and-white motor car. As he let in the clutch, there was a rattle as of small pebbles on a tin fence, and water in thin, broken lines crossed the smoky windscreen, beading, beating, lowering a curtain, till, within moments, the monsoon was over Uttar Pradesh. Biren switched the big headlamps on in irritation but there, blocking our way, stood a man in soaked shirt and darkening trousers, an arm raised to shut the blaze out of his eyes.

'It's Nilu,' said my father. 'Your Bela's brother.'

Another hearty cousin, I thought, lining up in my head the series of jocose and secretly neurotic young men (machismo and a forgettable variety of wit) who swam into our orbit from time to time and then vanished, mercifully never to return. The car rolled with a soft, muddy rustle and stopped beside the wet apparition.

'Where have you been?' said my father. 'I've been sitting with Sachi-mama for hours.'

'It's Biren-da, isn't it?' said an apologetic voice. 'I wish I hadn't left home. Won't you come in again ... just for a while?'

'No,' said my father. 'I've got to rush. A patient with a strangulated hernia may have called. It usually means surgery right away. Meet Megha here, my daughter ... Incidentally, when are you coming to meet Ratna? She was asking about you. How about Sunday, twelve thirty-ish?'

'I'll be there,' replied the man in the liquescent dark, coming over to my side and patting my cheek wetly through the window.

He stood watching as the car reversed and turned and gathered speed, on and on, as if it were the most natural thing to dress up and stand in the rain of an evening. He looked as if he had always been there ... And in the more accessible lobes of my brain, there lingers to this day the image of an arm raised to cover the eyes, a body arching, drenched, at the mercy of heraldic car lamps, while the rain, the battering, soaking, form/dissolving rain, falls out of a prodigal sky.

Biren and Ratna (whom, to tell my story simply, I must call by their first names) lived with my brother, Sujit, and me in a sunless, four/bedroom house with trailing money/plant, phenyl/scented floors, and big windows with wire netting in them. The lamps indoors were bright, and the curtains chosen to match the floral print on the sofas that had scallops on the back, edged with a pretty pink. In the evenings, when we came home from school, Ratna always waited with a hot meal, poories and a mutton curry. She watched over our homework, sent us out to play in the neighbourhood and put us to bed each night by nine. No mornings, on the other hand, were ever successfully crossed without her steaming, swelling and exploding in a series of small rages between eleven and lunchtime. They were usually of little consequence, if aimed at the cook, the ayah, the mali (each of whom had inevitably neglected or overdone something), Sujit and me (for skipping baths or lessons or making an infernal din), all in one day. We heard from her most about what was wrong with Biren, our closer relatives and her friends, and in the end – while Sujit and I grew up watching grown/ups closely, intensely, with adult eyes – the burden of the world's short/comings wore us out a bit.

Sujit was three years younger than I, with his hair cut so short, you could see each bristle stand up black and separate. Indoors, we played checkers or hide/and/seek with the servants, or hung for hours from large wooden hooks in an inner verandah, dreaming we were on the trapeze. We loved the circus. Somehow, by the end of each day of play, I had invariably managed to offend Sujit (I teased, I know, and attracted attention, asking too many meddlesome questions, but surely there was some other reason). For when Ratna and Biren were out for dinner, we fought as two possessed, with belts, dogs' chains, chairs or whatever came to hand till the servants parted us or one of us ran away. The rest of the time, Sujit paid little attention to people; he spent his days dreaming inside the family car as it stood outside, practising the shifts from clutch to gear to accelerator till the movements turned into reflexes, talking to himself all the while. On summer afternoons, he would crouch for hours under the bed with a long stick, making believe that he was a humorous, paan-chewing taangwala, who told his customers small anecdotes as he took them around the bazaars of a city: Agra, Lucknow, Allahabad. If at times he could be persuaded to stop talking to himself and actually listen to you, Sujit opened his eyes very wide, rubbing two enormous deckle-edged front teeth against his lower lip.

On the Sunday following my visit to Bela, Sujit and I sat on the dining-room floor, covering a carrom board with talcum powder, making it fly into each other's noses. Ratna was screaming at the cook for leaning her best dinner china out to dry against the kitchen door when Biren parted the curtains and let a visitor into our private disharmonies:

'Look who's arrived,' he announced to Ratna. 'D'you recognize him? It's Nilu, Sachi-mama's son.' It was the apparition of a few evenings ago, only he was controlled and tidy and adult this time, not melting away into dark water.

Ratna's face, which had been white with fury a moment ago, coloured with pleasure. 'He's all grown up,' she said.

'I saw him years ago, for his thread ceremony. He must have been all of fifteen. And precocious, my, ripe beyond his years.'

The guest stood silent as he was discussed, his raincoat covering the clean floor with a row of curly-edged puddles. Sujit and I didn't like grown-ups. They joked and patted you, and asked (loudly) questions to which they already had answers. Above all, they moved and spoke so grandly when, in fact, they understood nothing. Nothing at all. We noted the puddles and examined the visitor from a small distance. He spoke little and looked into Sujit's face and mine with expectation, as if we counted for something. As if he was guessing who we were. We weren't going to tell him; all the same, it was odd how he looked ... grave and piercingly. The raincoat came off. There were beautifully stitched trousers and a cream shirt beneath. He watched everything with half-closed eyes.

It's a vice I've inherited from my parents; we're suckers, even Sujit, for beauty in the corporeal frame, and before us stood a creature with a slow musical voice, an oriental Paul Newman with an open face, whose nostrils turned translucent when he laughed ... Every evening after that, he came over to the house (those warm, quickened, magical evenings), dragging one leg slightly behind the other as he crossed the street, self-conscious as an athlete, and as perfect. Something curious happened to Sujit and me each time we spotted him. Our brains snapped shut to whatever it was we were doing and we were grabbed instead by an imperative, an urgent plucking, just as if he had actually called out. Sujit and I would detach ourselves quietly, without a pang, from a cluster of whooping children at rounders or cricket and walk with gathering speed to confront this threat of glamour that had loped so recently into our lives.

When we were fully acquainted, the visitor gave me puzzles to do (with numbers and matchsticks) and asked me questions of 'general knowledge'. I hated the questions but the manner of his asking, the close attention (and his full, curved mouth) got its hook firmly into me. As if the right answer would touch a button, a secret spring, and open up a small, verdant realm at any moment, a state of grace, to which just the two of us would be privy ... When he tried with Sujit, the lazy brute made a rude noise, rolled his eyes and answered 'America' to all questions. Which is when Nilukaka (for that is how we called him) began to tell Sujit about tanks and anti-aircrafts guns, camouflage and the manoeuvres of war. Sujit sat close beside him, his mouth open, touching from time to time his shoes with his own.

Basically, I don't like families. I discovered that quite early. For just as you've finished peeling your warm boiled egg and are sprinkling it with salt and pepper or are quietly putting your school books away or even just beginning a small daydream about boarding school, somebody close by will start a tantrum. Your father hissing venom over misplaced papers, your mother's red face and look of hatred turned to you, accusing, demanding, even your little brother revealing sudden resentment or laying blame at your door ... I remember a foggy winter in Rampur, a small western district, when I was eight. We lived in a sprawling house, with acres of land about us, but finding all the bathrooms occupied one morning, I ran outside and squatted in a corner of the porch. Not a soul was around, and I watched with satisfaction a slow, curling trickle of water making its way down a slope. As I stood up, there loomed above me the figure of my father, speechless with rage. He took me to Ratna and described what he had seen. With exclamations of anger and incredulity, Biren asked me again and again why I had urinated out of doors, and for days afterwards, there lurked about the house an air of foreboding that had little to do with decency or a child's toilet training. Why were they so angry? Did Biren fear that I would grow up to be an exhibitionist, and place my privates on view for the world? I shall never know. What remains is a weekend of cowering from a father's anger that I did not understand, and a mother who failed to defend me.

So while Sujit ran off to the boys in the servants' quarters to tug at sugarcane with his teeth, and climb trees or the backs of buffaloes, while he played marbles like a maniac through the day, I would sit in a small room making up tunes on a harmonium that grew in complexity each morning. In the winters, I bought a small gift from the local exhibition, face powder or a picture of the English queen that I carefully mounted on cardboard and handed to my mother (months later) for her birthday. I wrote poems to her as well, storing them up in a small wooden chest together with the gift I had bought.

They were beautiful mornings, cold, crisp, my coat pocket full of dry fruit, my head of imaginings of the sleek and wise adult I would grow up to be, who would have the effect of calming everybody around her. (The woman in question was always tall, with dark hair and painted lips, in a georgette sari. She would stand in one place, welcoming but silent, and everybody would want to talk to her.) I had other pleasures, namely the books that Ratna got for me, and I read *The Hound of the Baskervilles* one December night when I was alone in the huge Rampur house with its creaks and whispers, and a certain moaning in the fog outside. (Ratna and Biren were out for a late dinner and Sujit in the servants' quarters with his friends, eating bajra rotis before a leaping fire.) I lay under a quilt, tense and thrilling to the bay of a spectral hound on some foggy, moonlit moor, turning up the radio towards the end for a clearer sound of human voices. It was a delicious time, it was a solitary time, and while our parents took Sujit and me out quite often, speaking to us on a variety of subjects (mainly during meals), I do not remember Sujit and me saying anything to them at all.

When this story begins, Biren was thirty-five years old and teaching surgery at the Allahabad Medical College, talented, crazy about his profession, and with fingers of deft magic. He had the shortest temper of all the people I have known, and wet his arms right up to his elbows, making much lather, every time he washed his hands. Earlier, for many years, he had left us with Ratna's parents so that he could gather up a number of degrees from the West, and wherever he turned now, there gathered about him people with dreaded illnesses, disorders of pelvis or thorax, that craved an awl-like intelligence to prod them coldly about, but one they felt sure would transform their sluggish tortured bodies in the end with a swift, minor miracle.

He frightened us very much at times. As on that evening, when Ratna, Sujit and I were returning from a day trip to Rewa, a town nearby. We had gone in the motor car of Ratna's friend, a woman doctor, who had some official work to attend to in the course of our visit. It took longer than expected, and we were several hours late coming into Allahabad. It was getting dark with the city still miles away. Suddenly, every five kilometres or so, we began to be stopped by police cars. There was an ambulance. The doctor with us began to show signs of alarm. The police were asking about a Srimati Lahiri, my

9

mother. Has there been an accident? Is anybody hurt? What held you up on the way? We arrived home at last, escorted by jeeps with monstrous wailing sirens. Before the house were gathered all the doctors of the city, some three hundred, in varying stages of mourning. Biren had left nobody out. Ratna slipped in quietly through a side gate while the police talked to the guests ... nothing had happened, everybody was safe. When Biren was angry, he never raised his voice. He murmured, as Sujit and I heard him murmur that evening to Ratna in the dining room. All at once, there was the sound of two dinner plates hitting the further, neon-lit brick wall one after another, and Ratna crying out tearfully, 'Stop it, stop this mad-ness,' followed by Biren walking briskly in the direction of his car, to return again only after midnight ... In the morning, after his bath, we would hear him sing a thumri, resonantly, trying out difficult notes. He had a lovely voice.

CHAPTER TWO

Into those sticky summer evenings (for two successive years) walked Nilu Haldar, a gentle, unintending breeze, with rain upon its wing. With Biren away on his evening rounds, Nilu would arrive around six and sit quietly in a cane chair, watching Ratna plait tightly her thick, black hair and frown in fear of her own youth, her glowing skin and the unmistakable attention they received. It must have been nice, for Nilukaka didn't speak very much. It was the manner of his listening as Ratna gently ranted, his eyes following her every gesture of hand or eye, that told Ratna she was beautiful. Sujit and I hung about, meanwhile, allowing not a glance or phrase of the man to escape our greedy eyes and ears. In an emotional sense, Ratna was really quite exhausted in those days, with little further to give, that is, after Biren's tireless sexual demands, his demand always, all the time, of perfection from her. She tended the home and each of us briskly, with a keen dutifulness, scatty but covering much ground. Recently, of nights, the house had started to settle into a profound sulk as Biren began heading off with regularity to the Cosmopolitan Club ... he was getting to like his drink. They would be evenings of Ratna muttering, flinging her combs, Sujit in tears, as the sediment of a large-sized gloom settled slowly in our separate chests.

Nilu neither smoked nor drank, he seemed free and hard and unbroken. Nothing would ever defeat him. Ratna suggested that for a man of his generation, such habits of austerity were a kind of posturing. Or worse, they signified a need for everybody's approval:

'How's it I never see you take a cigarette or a drink from Biren?' she asked. 'One can hardly get by without these little aids in your profession. How does one survive those endless Mess parties? Maybe you keep off the stuff when you come home, to show respect to elders, that sort of thing?' Her face went red for she wasn't much older at all.

Nilu's eyes closed a little further, crinkling with amusement. 'Do I?' he said. 'If you ask me, I truly envy people who like their drink. It doesn't turn the world all rosy and right side up for me, in fact, it doesn't do anything at all. So I sit like a dull hog, watching others light up with love for the world or drowning in the blackest despair, all through the use of a stimulant. They don't, incidentally, make a pretty sight.'

'It's not just that,' interposed Ratna, uncertain whether to approve the high tone or laugh it away, 'but the way you eat as well. Next to nothing, picking at the good food before you as though eating's the last thing you want to do.'

'Which is probably right,' he laughed. 'Most of the time, I hardly notice what I'm given. Such wonderful things usually at hand to watch or listen to, I eat because I must.'

I looked at his gleaming, muscular forearm, its fine golden hairs. Maybe that was the way you got when you were twenty-five. Sujit and I were always looking for food.

Though she grumbled endlessly about inessentials, Ratna never really told Nilu how her life with Biren was fraught, about the anxiety of being on trial every day, but he guessed and put it all to rights in a few moments each evening with his soft voice, his tribute of attention.

One afternoon, I returned from school and found Ratna standing at the door. As we went in, she said, disturbed, confiding:

'I told him today. When he came in the morning, I told him.'

'Whom?' I asked. 'What did you say?'

'Your Nilukaka,' replied my mother. 'Funny habit the man has, dropping in to see me in the mornings, when all of you are away. He probably doesn't mean any harm, of course.'

I nodded, so he came round each morning. 'What did you say to him?' I asked Ratna.

'It's nice of you to come by, I said, but you know your Biren-da. So quick to leap to conclusions. Would you mind coming over in the evenings, when he and the children are around? We so look forward to seeing you.'

'And he, what did he say?' I was shocked that this finest of relatives, the exquisite Nilukaka, had been given a put-down. As if he could ever have any but the right intention. Did I do right, asked my mother, and at thirteen (when I could scarcely know that from the earliest times, whenever there had been a man and woman in a story, one of them had always had the wrong intention), I was struck with tragedy at the attribution of foul motive to Nilukaka.

'He took it like a gentleman,' answered Ratna. '"Certainly, boudi," he said, "from now on, I shall come in only after six. I didn't intend to embarrass you . . . I hope you believe that?"'

I liked his silences, the way his mouth worked when he listened to either Biren or Sujit. He seldom interrupted and in the end, when his own speech came, euphonic and low, we listened (each of us) with the full might of our concentration rolled up into the act. For no word was free of reflection, and he silenced unreasoning anger or feelings of injury with a powerful, soft glove. With Sujit and me, he was very physical. He arm-wrestled, he held my hand when I spoke to him and, whenever we met, he hugged both of us. Which blew the lid off our world, left us in a permanent daze. For Bengali families don't hug, they instruct and improve.

Often, as he arrived, Nilukaka would switch on the big radio in the sitting room, filling the house with the adenoidal moos and loving yews and I-ain't-gonnas of Pat Boone and Elvis Presley. They sounded silly to me, but the lines always rhymed and the kids in school were crazy about them, so when Nilukaka put Sujit's head and mine close to the amplifier, we listened just in case the sounds suddenly began to mean something. (Actually, the man just wanted to be left alone to talk to Ratna, safe from the stares of two greedy children who missed absolutely no expression on his countenance.) Soon it would be bedtime for Sujit and me, and 'A Date With You' coming over the wires, with Captain Rajiv sending 'his fondest love to the girl who is listening reluctantly', asking her to forgive him. Or birthday wishes from Gopi, Karuna, Ratty, Pattie and Bunny, who hoped that 'Johnny's recent jaundice won't come in the way of his drinking half a bottle of the good stuff to celebrate the evening'. Then music and, again, the crackling, over-bright quips of a callow compère ... Nilukaka taught me to cha-cha, off-beat, he called it; that and the quickstep. If we jived, I unfailingly scuffed his shoes and bumped against his chest, so very soon, with my self-respect under siege, I'd run off ... I noticed then his clothes' mild smell of sweat, his beautiful, prominent bottom.

When Biren came home, the conversation instantly sat up into the clipped, humorous tongue of a man talking to another, self-important, heavy with fact and, not seldom, snide as hell. The favoured subject that summer was Britain's hapless Minister for Defence, John Profumo, and his piquant carnal life with the charming Christine Keeler. As the season grew and further bits flowed in from across the sea, the voices got lower, the eyes hotter, as Miss Keeler rose from the many-coloured vapours of a West End bathtub to throw her fragrant towel to a whewing, dry-throated audience. Nilu usually plied Biren with tidbits on the defence scandal, the putative secrets now with the Russians ... I devoured the intense, sly, delighted faces of the two, picking up from where I stood (by the dining table) the smell of sex and the knowledge of its power over men. Before long, Biren would notice my attention, my evident, dazzled understanding, and with a sibilant puff on his cigarette, order me out of the room. It was mildly unsettling, being dismissed in that way, but I waited in the next room till it was eight thirty, when the grown-ups would drive off to the club. I then emptied out a desk in the guest room that held a supply of the month's *Blitz*. There in my shaking fingers it would lie, the length of a long, pearly nude with black-painted nails and eyelid, Keeler or Mandy Rice-Davies in yogic pose, or bending backwards with a hand partly covering the crotch. I devoured with gathering speed stories of gymnastics in the swimming pool and shows for peeping toms; I learned about the smouldering lives in more than one country that the two ladies fanned to flame ... It was mentioned somewhere that the thing Christine K. best inspired in the men of her acquaintance was love. They said she would marry a baronet.

Ten thousand pilgrims, announced the radio one evening, were preparing to descend upon the city in the autumn and bathe at the confluence of the Ganga and the Yamuna. Wash off the sins of many lives, remarked Biren, an irreverent man, and all the germs of their infected flesh into the city's water supply. Primitive bloody crea-tures. Then with the speed of a man of imagination, his ability to surprise, he said, let's go for a swim up the river tomorrow. Before sunrise. It's a Sunday, so we can eat a lazy breakfast by the riverside. Nilu murmured that he had no bathing trunks.

Biren laughed aloud. 'Bathing trunks for the Ganga, that's blasphemy. Be a devil, get what you have. We pick you up in the morning at five.'

That night, Sujit and I slept beside our parents on a terrace verandah. There was a crash of thunder around two and I sat up to watch a thrilling bolt of lightning shoot from one corner of the night to another, in sudden candescence behind startled puffs of cloud. In my brain, as I lay down again, appeared Nilukaka's muscular back as it would be next day without a shirt, hard but with dents that made you feel weak just thinking about them. A beautiful rump ... the curved flesh would show pinkly through wet, white drawers. I thought then of my own breasts, little buds of flesh, would they show through the slip? There it was again, a firm, angular jaw, his eyes reddening with river water, and the swell of a deep male chest with little hairs clinging wetly to it. My breath was coming faster. I felt a warmth on my face and palms, my inner leg. I felt that something (an idea, a bud, a chained beast) would burst forth that night, there would be a riot, an uncontrollable effusion ... The rain came finally in bursts and was resonant on the aluminium roof for the rest of the night. My toes were getting the spray. I drew them in, tucking the drawsheet tightly about my legs, against the bewitchment of the monsoon and its inevitable Indian concomitant, desire. It was morning before I slept.

At the riverside, it was a clear, rainless day with the clang and peal of temple bells from a series of dark recesses and kirtan singing by a drugged, early-morning voice over the microphones to a rasping, half-tuned harmonium. We dipped jalebis in hot milk at a wooden table covered with the circular traces of tea drunk by thousands of pilgrims before us, and graffiti (in a very uninspired Hindi) always about one female part. Sujit roused himself to examine these artefacts closely from time to time, and read them aloud to Nilu ... I wanted to gag and beat him. Immersed waist-deep near the bank were a score of men and women, chanting, offering their libation of milk or water to the sun. A petal-ridden, sandalwood-smeared, incense-stoked scene of a terrific self-absorption ... A corpulent priest bullied some villagers for their offering (where was the money, he wanted to know), and a cry rose in praise of Mahadev as cold water shocked an unwoken skin. The sun rose unhurried and pink, bathing first the water, a few clouds and a part of the sky with its wasteful, warm, freshly mixed salmon colour. Within moments, it lost patience, however, and turned into the old blinding dazzle in the height of the sky, leaving the water cool, pure and wavy with a thousand uncompleted reflections.

Sujit and I kicked our way through the sand to watch

rows of squatting men getting hair shaved from their heads, chins, armpits, the glistening bared strips. Thin barbers dipping grey razors into aluminium mugs and cleaning the victim's proffered part expertly, with pursed mouths. A boatman rowed us up the Ganga ... I was sitting beside him, splashing Sujit's flinching face with river water when a small, cloth-wrapped bundle floated sociably towards us, and Biren said I'd have to stop. It was a corpse in knee-high dhoti, with the head and feet under water, and a small, vulnerable bottom that kept bobbing up beside the boat in its dust-stained white cloth. Somebody's murdered the poor sod, said Biren. I felt suddenly lonely and abandoned in a way I felt sure the drowned man must feel, and the bleakness would not go away till the boatman spoke up. Nobody cremates a man with snakebite, he said, for one day, the serpent that smote him returns and gazes into his dead eyes. If the man is around, it usually bites him back to life.

Finally, there was the confluence and Biren pointing to the clear, iron waters of the Yamuna as they slid past the Ganga, muddy, opaque, blessed. He entered the water quickly and floated away on his back, unmindful of germs. Nilukaka hung beside the boat for a while (there were white drawers), turning over in his mind the wages of doing something pleasantly barbaric, bathing in the holy waters. Sujit, who was not yet a swimmer, leaped in after the men with a swashbuckling readiness and emerged at once, a gasping, sneezing, water-spattering fowl. I stood in the boat, clutching a white slip to my neck, till Biren bobbed up and pulled me in, laughing, ducking my head again and again into the awful grey surge. My breasts (they were just swollen brown nipples to begin with) showed clear and outraged through the cotton slip. Then

Nilu began a slow, transfixing crawl two hundred yards up the river (right arm, left arm, head to left shoulder) that Ratna and I watched from the boat, a grace and quiet strength beyond our reach, beyond the faltering fancy . . . a coppery, hard body. He stood at last beside the boat, tousled, dripping, greedy for our approval.

We were home by the afternoon. It was warm for the month of September, and Sujit and I were nearing the end of a brief autumn vacation. After lunch, Ratna went in for a nap and Biren sat in the white glare of the afternoon windows, reading his Sunday papers. Nilukaka was at the table, parrying with Sujit, who boxed him fitfully in the stomach and shoulders. I stood watching the two through the corner of my eye, hoping that I looked sufficiently mysterious and worthy of attention for Nilukaka to seek me out. In a moment, he lifted his red face out of a clinch with Sujit and asked me something . . . what was it? I'd been waiting for him to speak all along, but when it came, the invitation to join in, I missed it. He asked his question again. Again (for the cobwebs that caught in between), I failed to hear, and became in consequence more remote, even haughty, in the profile I turned to him. My throat was dry, I was getting a little anxious. Nilu smiled, incredulous and coaxing now, speaking the question more slowly, but the more I stared at his full mouth, the words they formed, the further all of it receded, becoming another language, becoming gibberish. I first stared blindly into a magazine, then began to edge slowly out of the room. Biren, so far immersed in dull, black print, pushed the rustling sheets aside. He gritted his teeth:

'Are you dumb?' roared the man. 'Don't you know what to do when spoken to by a grown-up? Answer him. Now, you ill-mannered girl.'

From a great distance, I felt my mouth open to say that I hadn't heard him, but no sound came. Sujit stood beside me motionless.

'What, what was that you said?' (A great muscled beast with stripes and bared fang that I encountered only during sleep was there, striding firmly in through the door. The fright, and hairs bristling up on my back.) Biren gritted still his uneven, tobacco-stained teeth. 'I'll teach you to reply to your elders, to show respect, if I have to use . . .'

'I merely asked,' plunged Nilu, alarmed, urging me with nods, 'when it is that Megha's school reopens. Autumn vacation should be over soon.'

It was hard to get the words out of my mouth since so little of me remained in the room.

'The fifth of October,' I whispered. 'October five.'

He was reading his newspapers again. I must have left the room. My feet ran through several rooms to a place far away. I stopped in an enclosure (dark, concealing) formed by two box pelmets facing different ways. They began to tremble, my legs below the knees, my arms, my shoulders, fingers, face, chest, all of them shook in a kind of convulsion . . . In the purlieus of the afternoon, I sensed a man parting the curtain to kneel on the floor before me. He took me in his arms, holding me tightly to his chest till the trembling (slowly, altogether) ceased. I fell, a throbbing, blood-covered foetus through an airless tunnel, gasping and then still . . . I had wanted so much that this magnificent grown-up should think me serious, graceful, able to cope. Now, I was a clod of earth, kicked to a thousand homeless particles before him by Biren. I was a

20

clod. When I was quiet (at least, on the outside) Nilukaka looked gravely into my eyes:

'You can't mind what Biren-da says,' he pleaded. 'Everybody knows his temper, he forgets himself. This time, he was definitely in the wrong, maybe even he knows it . . . I'm sorry I caused the eruption, but look at it this way: it could have been me he was saying all those things to. It could, you know. He's perfectly capable.'

Slowly, in what was still dead sandy soil, and not open to much cajolement, a small, stringy plant took root . . . A scene with him, Nilu, the invincible fair knight, suffering this humiliation at somebody's hands . . . that it could, if one turned it over in one's mind, happen to others. And some of the sordidness went away, some of the shame. I was breathing calmly now, watching Nilu-kaka without a word till Sujit joined us, picking his nose, that marvellous connector of wild, nameless agonies with the magic of quotidian detail, the tiny hairs on his head bristling and curious.

CHAPTER THREE

Two o'clock. Damyanti lifted the curtain, really a green-and-white checked bedspread hung on the front door, and saw her husband pant briskly up the road to the house. She retreated indoors. Women who stood at front doors, said Beni Madho, were women on the look-out. For fresh pasture, men, he meant. Damyanti usually came out to chase the cows, gentle, greedy creatures that put their noses in the front door. Or to beckon to the vegetable man, a laughing one-eyed cheat, to bring the yam or jackfruit to the back of the house, where they could chaffer amicably without all Colonelgunj getting to know what Misra's wife was feeding him that afternoon.

Damyanti was born in the middle 'twenties when young men were putting on white caps to join the Mahatma's marches. Her mother was less sure in which month the spiritless child had quit her womb. In the summer, she once said after a superhuman effort of memory, but in a country with eight months of heat, the pundits had found the intelligence less than satisfactory. No horoscope could be cast for the girl. She was lucky, that much was clear, for a Saryupari Brahmin, BA, who was visiting her father, had espied the girl, wordless as a moth amongst her chattering sisters, and asked for her hand in marriage.

That was when her plait had swung down to her knee and her breasts bloomed so round that her father forbade her to leave the house. Now, in 1970, with her temples going lightly grey, she could go to the market if she wished, said Beni Madho, for it was only the young ones men looked at. In the early days, Damyanti had sung bits of thumri as she did the chores (her mother had trained her voice), but singing and those coloured magazines spelt evil for women, said Beni Madho. They made their minds languid and intemperate.

He walked up a road tarred and brilliant in the heat, beside a line of unpainted, blackening houses, Beni Madho Misra, Saryupari Brahmin. He wiped a weak, swarthy face on a towel with woven yellow snakes as he entered the cheerless, high-roofed house left to him by his father. Beni Madho taught Commerce at the Government Hindi High School, what he saw as an ill-paid struggle to get some order into the scattered, scheming minds of a bunch of nameless hoodlums who would never amount to much anyway. He taught (with much brandishings of stick) a changeless, enervating syllabus that had sucked flat in twenty years his keen and cynical brain.

Without a word, he took a clean dhoti and vest held out by his wife, and hanging the sacred thread from his ear, entered the bathroom's cool gloom. Lifebuoy soap and Brahmi Amla hair oil. Beni Madho rubbed his scalp vigorously, then squatting widely like a woman, sluiced the popped pores of his summer skin with grey water from iron buckets. Soon afterwards, he was eating rice with daal and bhindi out of a brass thali in the kitchen, its walls as black as a nightmare, while Damyanti stood by, fanning him. And each time he looked up, she ladled out more rice, papad, pickle on to his plate without a word being said on either side.

23

'Next week,' he said, belching gently, 'we'll have a lodger in the upstairs room.' He had threatened this for many years, but each time somebody, his brother or the principal of his school, had talked him out of it.

'Upstairs,' muttered Damyanti. 'Where Bapu lived all those years. I've kept his things exactly as they were when he was alive, the dhotis and walking stick. To have a stranger lie on his bed now . . . how would Bapu feel?'

'It's two years since the old man died,' observed Beni Madho drily. 'How long will our cheek stay wet with tears?'

'Nothing,' said Damyanti, 'is sacred or out of reach for you. It's a wonder you didn't bring a tenant in while he was still alive.'

'Quiet, woman. Do you think a schoolmaster's pay will feed a household in these days? There's the electricity, the water. Bapu lived in a golden age when, on two hundred rupees, you could support a family of six. And keep a cow, and servants.'

'So could you,' she retorted, tying and untying a knot in her sari, 'if you weren't throwing your money away on . . . on other things. What are our expenses, anyway? I do all the work this house needs.'

He pushed away his thali, which banged against the wall, water from a brass tumbler fanning across the rough kitchen floor. The illogicality of women. Giving them an education was no answer, it just made them more clamorous. He limped to a hand-pump in the courtyard, his hard melon-belly heaving before him, and spewed a noisy, practised column of water into the drain.

'Think about it,' she pleaded, rustling the leaves of his brain back to the present, the irritant of wedlock. 'Do you want a man in the place where you've hidden your wife for so many years? He might enter the courtyard when I bathe or dry my hair in the sun . . . have you lost all caution?'

Beni Madho laughed, nasty and soft, picking his teeth. 'You should look into a mirror some time,' he said. 'You'll find a small-mouthed, hag-ridden woman who never laughs, and in the presence of people, turns as silent as cattle. What lodger would take a fancy to you unless he were both blind and deaf?' Under his breath, he muttered, 'Everybody's not the fool Beni Madho was when he married.'

He didn't have to say it, thought Damyanti, she knew only too well what a spent and nerveless thing she was, who never said clever, prophetic things about ministers or corruption or the price-rise. 'I don't want to wash his clothes,' she declared, in sudden despair. 'Or wait up for him when he's late. He might ask for bath water to be carried up to the terrace.'

'You'll do as he says, mend his clothes, clean his dirt, and no more argument. I have fed you so many years, and I haven't even a son to look after me in my old age.' Her face closed as if he'd slapped her. Beni Madho continued: 'He's going to pay well, five hundred rupees for the room alone . . . It's a university lecturer, just returned from vilayat. A gentilman.'

Beni Madho switched on the fan and stretched himself out on an easy-chair in the front room. Guiltily, with a child's powerless hands, Damyanti pressed his legs down from the middle of the thigh to the ankle, to the sole of the foot. She had given him no child. At forty-six years now, she never would give him one . . . In a while, his head rolled to the side, and a snore with uneven whistles filled the room. His wife returned to the kitchen with dead eyes, to eat what was left by Beni Madho.

In a while, she saw him enter the bedroom, humming under his breath, and change into a white kurta with crinkling sleeves. He had lately acquired sideburns on his ripe, purple cheek, into which he now rubbed a green pomade from a bottle with a gold cap. Next, he dabbed something on his chest, his thick, grey neck and behind the ears with a tender calculation. It was the ittar of rose.

Damyanti sprang up in the kitchen, fingers drying fast, and stood trembling in sections of her arms, stomach, thighs. In a moment, Beni Madho had swung the gathers of a new, starched dhoti over his arm and singing softly (My bracelet, it keeps slipping off, my lover hath cast a spell upon me) walked fleshily out of the door. In a mirror that hung in the verandah, he had taken a last deep look into his eyes ... Damyanti fought back the tears, and ran to the front room to see him walk, first slowly, then with gathering speed, up the brutal, dazzling tar from the house. Who was it now, she wondered, her eyes dimming. Always, that is, soon after the first two years of marriage, there had been some playful, laughing woman to make Beni Madho a paan for his tobacco and do other unthinkable things with. Yet even now, when he left for a tryst, Damyanti felt in his exit a sharp, obliterating kick to her stomach and bow-shaped mouth, her still-youthful round breasts. Another woman might have screamed at him and flung off her mangalsutra, the symbol of binding matrimony. Damyanti simply stood there, waves of nausea, grief, loneliness surging up in her breast and refusing, just refusing, to recede. She throbbed, a butterfly freshly stamped on, slipping breath by painful breath to a quietus. She knew (since he did not care) that when he returned in the evening, she would still say nothing, and the tears in her throat would dry up into a necklace of hard, little seeds. She went back to washing the kitchen things.

One morning, Beni Madho returned early from school. Damyanti had finished her bath, and was watering the little tulsi sapling in the courtyard with a small, bronze lota. As she lowered her praying eyes, there came a clatter of hooves on the road, a long hot neigh and boxes that came thudding dully to the ground. Beni Madho ran out, and entered the courtyard a moment later with a large suitcase, four cardboard boxes bursting rudely with books, nylon bags and a brightly coloured rush mat. A young man, the hair falling into his eyes, stood wiping his spectacles. Beni Madho was doing a little dance around the luggage, two steps forward, one back; he smiled without ceasing and was full of English words that morning. The young man spoke Hindi. From a distance, he joined his hands in salutation to Damyanti, who looked away. He wore blue jeans and a white khaddar kurta. The men made their way up the stairs.

For a few days, Beni Madho took the lodger's meals up to his room, then tired swiftly of his mime of the good-natured landlord . . . he was becoming late for his evening calls. The lodger began to come down to the kitchen when he was hungry. He spoke to Damyanti a few times, how near is the nearest cinema, where do I buy shoe polish, but her silence was not for breaking. She arranged what she cooked neatly on his thali — he was paying, wasn't he — and passed the meal wordlessly in his direction. He also came down before dusk sometimes, and sat drinking tea by himself in the courtyard.

One morning, Damyanti returned from the market to find him emerging from the bathing room.

'I was in there washing my clothes,' said the lodger, handing greyish, twisted coils to Damyanti. 'I thought I'd wash yours and Misraji's as well.'

Damyanti was offended. Wordlessly, she took the clothes and hung them up on the line, shaking each to take the creases out. To go in like that and waste water, must have finished off the soap, too.

He seemed to read her thoughts. 'Where I come from in England, it was a crime to waste water. You put a little coin into a machine for a bath.'

Damyanti was not appeased. Stranger interfering in the running of my household . . . as if, had he asked, I'd have refused to wash his clothes. Making a woman look small.

'It's better this way,' he suddenly said, pulling his moustache, watching her with a small smile. 'You go to the market and do the outdoor things, and I'll clean up for you . . . whenever I'm free. Men can be tired of having to go out all the time.'

He was an odd fellow but he seemed to want to talk. Beni Madho would never have said that, even in joke. I'll clean up for you. Never.

She went upstairs one evening while the men were away. There were books stacked neatly on shelves, a lamp and a small radio, and a bed made carefully on the floor . . . So he wasn't sleeping on Bapu's bed.

Urmila, her friend, lived in the house next door. One afternoon, as Damyanti waited for Beni Madho, she heard Urmila scream, and then her husband's voice, hoarse, accusing . . . In a moment, he came down the front steps, pulling Urmila after him by the hair. She fell on her knees, holding her head, but her hair was wrapped in a coil round his hand, and he pulled it again and again. Damyanti came out of her door, trembling, her voice gone, then she saw the lodger. He leaned his arm calmly, insolently, on Urmila's gate.

'Any problem, bhaisaheb?' he asked, without raising his voice. 'The lady seems to be in distress. I think you'd better leave her alone or I shall call the police. I went to school with this town's SP, you know.'

The man's face went black with rage; meddlesome young swine, I'll make him forget his father's name. Then understanding swooped, mercurial, ready to rescue. His features assumed a placatory, embarrassed expression, if not without a struggle: 'Heen heen, it's the vilayati babu,' he said. 'Actually, you've misunderstood us. I was just explaining something to her, this woman keeps trying to pick a quarrel ... You look tired today, babuji.' Damyanti slipped indoors to warm the young man's food.

Another morning, she sat in the yard, cleaning rice for the afternoon. The lodger leaned from the terrace and said with a terrible irrelevance: 'I'm on holiday this week. I think I'll run off and meet some relatives who not only dislike me but will be quite put out by my arrival.'

When she looked up, Damyanti saw lowered before her (on threads) a set of toy ducks, bright yellow with wide black eyes, and beaks that opened and shut. Quack quack, said the forward little birds, waddling indomitably back and forth. She began to laugh. Slowly, he descended the stairs, holding at his breast a carved wooden box with a roof and painted eaves, and some hanging chains and cobs. Ashwin Krishna, her husband had called him.

'It's a cuckoo clock,' he said. 'When it strikes one, this door opens and a little brown bird, no relation to those ducks, hops out and says "cuckoo". You wind it like this.

I bought it for my mother . . . Would you keep it in your room for a while?'

She was confused how to say it, in what words to refuse, since the fellow had come from England, so she took it from him quietly.

'Those little ducks are for a niece. My sister's child.'

Suddenly, unbidden, it came out, taking Damyanti herself by surprise: 'Where is your wife? Is she with your parents?'

He laughed soundlessly, tilting his head back. 'God help me, no. I don't want to be married yet, I'm only twenty-seven. And this is my first job. I teach history, did you know, at the university. There's so much I have to do before I settle down.'

'But your parents,' she probed, taken further aback. 'Where do they live? Why have they let you come to Allahabad?'

'They live in Benares. My father is a poet, a famous man. I thought of writing poetry, too, in the beginning, except I felt one had to teach the young in this country to feed themselves first. Poetry comes after.'

She laughed. He spoke as if writing poems was a way of earning a living. It put you in mind of matted locks, an unclean kurta and jhola, and probably begging people for food. If you were a musician, on the other hand, there was something to that. Waistcoats of banarasi brocade, the rich calling you to dinner and saying 'wah wah' to whatever you sang. People seldom knew good music from bad . . . And there was the sarangi, its beautiful, tragic cry breaking through lighted windows into a dark garden outside, the last notes still shaking in the air.

'Which England you come from?' she finally asked the odd, humorous young man.

'I come from an England called Oxford, mausi,' he

replied, smiling all over his narrow face. He had called her 'aunt', he was all right.

She wondered what Beni Madho would say. An ignorant nanny-goat, he would call her, for talking to a man from England, and her knowing neither *cat* nor *bat* nor *mat* of English. Where was Beni Madho this holiday, she wondered. He should have been lying on the veran-dah, cursing the neighbour's radio. He'd been coming home later and later these last evenings ... what woman was it this time? When he entered the house, Beni Madho had begun to give off a nauseous, sweet smell. Whoever it was had led him finally to liquor, the cesspit thing that Beni Madho had scorned all his fifty-one years.

CHAPTER FOUR

In the autumn of 1964, Biren was transferred to Benares, and shifted with Ratna to the place. Benares had poor schools, and since Ratna wanted a public school instruction for Sujit and me, we were sent back to Allahabad, to boarding schools this time. Where, since much of the world's knowledge was still available only in English, we would learn to think in that language, there would be sports in plenty, debate and theatre, and learning to stand up for yourself. Where the first general thoughts on morality, however laughable they might sound in the future, would be insinuated into our groping little minds by means of a subject called Moral Science.

I wouldn't have talked about school, the time when children are chiefly a mass of activity, netball, volleyball, prayers and prep and eating; where with so many peers about at once, all one wants is for the bell to go (for games or dinner) so that every thought nursed through the hours of silence (at prep or dorm) – and no matter its banality – can come pouring out in a great cascade before others of the same compulsion. There is, above all, the remorseless wish to belong, to love and hate the people and things that everybody else does ... children are the worst conformists. I want to talk about school for it revealed early an aspect of my life that doesn't take kindly to order or preciousness. Or prudery. And each time the going gets too straight, it has a way of obtruding with foul manners, drawing attention to itself, and all but wrecking the show. It came sneaking in unexpectedly in the form of a visitor to the convent, an old demon, but accompanied this time by a debilitating obsession for some of us. We'll come to that.

Sujit had never lived away from Biren and Ratna, and stood before the engine's sharp, enveloping mist at Benares station, refusing to look at his mother. I took him by the hand. Ratna had spent weeks folding and labelling a kit of shirts, socks, towels, sheets, handkerchiefs. Later, when people asked how I was coping with boarding school, great, said Ratna always. Megha never has a problem. In a way, she was right. All my life, however heartbreaking the circumstance, since I lacked love and never had the choice, I have managed very well. Strength, I want to say, is a matter of lacking options, the reasonable certainty that if you fall apart, there will be nobody about to pick up the pieces. So you put all you've got into never falling apart.

The school was run by German nuns, who if burningly sincere in bringing up right a gaggle of gleeful heathens, were without a trace of humour to lighten their grim burden. The girls didn't like me either when I was new. I was thin, with bushy eyebrows, and spotty from a recent chicken pox that caused a stir in any group I came to stand with. The girls' eyes acquired a pale, costive look as I arrived and they scattered suddenly, mindful of their chores. When I got better grades than them, and silver cups (for elocution or running a hundred metres), it put me in a distinctly bad light with the blonde, big-jawed, hundred-and-thirty pound Margaret Murray, who accosted me in a deserted gymnasium one evening, unhingeing my chin with her thick knuckle: 'I hear you say to people that I'm beefy and hopelessly dumb. Would you like to repeat the remark in my presence?' Then the girls discovered that I was always in trouble with the nuns – for talking after lights out in the dorm, or reading fiction all the way through prep. It did the trick, leaving them in no doubt that – whatever decencies I lacked – I had at least a heart of gold. So I learnt to make my bed tight as a cream roll, giving the snowy wick counterpane that extra tuck under the pillow, to wash my feet in a bowl of boiling water, and watch them go red before they were wiped and lifted into bed each night. At meals, I ate mountains of bread with mincemeat or boiled grey vegetables like the rest. And over the years, there grew between us an unshakeable warmth as we passed each other toilet paper during study and played sweaty, driven netball in the evenings. Nobody was allowed to sit out.

One Sunday, along with a dozen wild-haired, blazer-clad oglers from St Joseph's, the boys' school next door, Sujit was herded in to see me. We sat in the needlework room with its pink toy chairs and unnatural hush, the conversation never rising beyond a murmur. Two nuns sat in a corner of the room to ensure that we spoke only to our brothers, not to some unsettling swain going by the name of Marvin Bunting or Rudy D'Mello, with the greasy curled forelock of sedition, aftershave lotion and drainpipes. Sujit sat before me motionless, his head enormous on a thin body. His shoes hung huge and useless from the ankles, appurtenances of a rag doll.

'Have you learned to make your bed?' I asked. 'To cover your books with brown paper?' Sujit nodded, he was ten years old at the time.

'Are you doing your homework?' said I, with an officious thirteen-year-old's concern. He nodded again.

'How about friends? Do you have anyone to talk to at dinner and recreation? Do they rag you?'

Sujit's eyes were wild, unfocused. 'Have you something to eat?' he said. 'Anything. Biscuits, condensed milk, jam?'

I handed him first a bottle of strawberry jam I had saved up from my tuck. He produced a spoon from his pocket and swiftly, with the concentration of a surgeon, dug into and emptied the jar before him. Then he handed it back.

I gave him the condensed milk to take away. A nun rose, ringing a piercing little bell that summoned us to study. All through the day, after seeing Sujit, the faint patches on his cheeks and unwashed hair, I felt agitated. As if somewhere before me had been a statement of tragedy, an appeal to our ties of blood, and I had failed to grasp it.

Biren withdrew Sujit from Allahabad after a term. He sent him to Sherwood College in the hills, where they swam and rode ponies, and had glowing cheeks the year round from good food and the sharp Nainital air. Sujit, never a believer in the tonic powers of conversation, continued as he was, laconic but given to frenzied physical activity. It enabled him to excel in sport, particularly cricket, where he won the college colours as a batsman and wicket-keeper. He also took part in theatre at school, where – when he had to speak – it would always be as somebody else.

My mother said I managed like a dream, but I had a secret. I wet my bed. Not often or with memories of anguish, but every few months I would wake up in the small hours to a warm, seeping discomfort. It always frightened me. Would there be other urges, involuntary acts, madness later, that I would not be able to control? This one coincided always with a dream of lavatories, a series of them, and I seeking them out one by one. There were fouled ones, ones with broken seats, or just dark, scary holes that you could fall into. I would stop at none ... till at the end of an increasingly desperate search, there it would be, a large white-painted room in a colonial house with shining closet and rose-scented phenyl. Tenderly, I would lower the seat ... I haven't figured out (when the images of sleep leap so and bite) how other people tell a dream from the real thing. Why is it they don't wet their beds? Years later, though free of my affliction, I still have no answer.

We were very moral at school. On Sundays, Purry Singh (who was also the school genius) and I sat on a ledge, watching the Catholic girls go off to church, their gleaming socks and rakish angle of beret, their surreptitious, pale lipstick. In the choir, they would share their psalm books with the boys from St Joseph's, letting their silk blouses brush lightly the knobby elbows beside them. Purry and I decided we would never wear lipstick or high heels. For one thing led to another, there would be boys, then marriage, and then that awful thing in the dark. Some men even asked you to put your mouth there ... Lipstick was out.

Till in August one year, Captain Nilratan Haldar came to Allahabad on annual leave. A fact that his sister Bela, with the sly pleasure of one who understood my interest, my ardent interest, conveyed to me through a casual letter. As if on cue, my brain began to body forth and mix, not memories (too inconclusive the impressions

36

were for that) but a series of images, erupting⁄coalescing⁄
gone, of great physical beauty and gentleness. Above all,
gentleness. There were flashes too of rage and violent
gesture from Biren or Sujit, and always Nilukaka talking,
talking into the night. Taking Sujit away on a bicycle for
ice cream. Forcing − by the awl of an extreme beauty and
unction − the slow irruption of serenity and, before long,
laughter.

Sister Maria, a bouncing, broad⁄cheeked nun, came
one evening to the netball court and beckoned me
suspiciously to the parlour. I guessed who it was and
raced past several blocks of schoolrooms to a scented
enclosure with Louis Quinze chairs, a black⁄and⁄white
marble floor. Running quick fingers through my hair, I
entered the parlour, walking very slowly now. My cheeks
had a high colour when Nilu Haldar rose and embraced
me. It's you, I said, feigning a mild surprise as he looked
me over with a sharp curiosity. It was not the eyes that
held you, with their crinkling humorous folds, eyes that
continually appraised the object before them, but the way
his mouth worked, always saying something more than
was in fact spoken. He asked about Biren and Ratna, and
life at boarding school. All the time, I gave half⁄replies,
making mysteries where none existed. It was stepping once
again on uncommon ground, and in a stroke, the
sustaining details of my life, the games and anxious
friendships, the reading and acts of sacrifice for St Jude,
fell away from my centre, superfluous mud on a potter's
jar ... I waited for the next visit, in whose red kiln my
new⁄found shape could harden, be confirmed, and there
were several visits. Each time, I ran in red⁄faced from
rounders or basketball, anxious to display a calm that I
was far from feeling. He spoke of his regiment and the
girls he knew, he brought me books to read, Graham

Greene or Morris West, always with the lightness and caution of a twenty-seven-year-old with a child, but which left me — as in madness — with a growing incapacity for all the main activities of my life.

Sujit was down in Allahabad that year, and we went with Nilu to spend Dasshera with his parents, Sachi-mama and Mami. Sujit's attention to Nilu was total every moment he was with him, uncorrupted, that is, by any desire to conceal his love. Nilukaka would sit in a darkened room each evening, listening to jazz with his face in his hands. Sujit sat beside him unmoving, in an identical posture, a miniature of the older man. What sense Sujit made of musical discord or how he coped with the difficulty of listening to pure jazz for a whole evening, it is hard to say; it was his steadfastness and unflinching attention that was terrible to see.

In the mornings, Sujit and I would awaken to Nilu-kaka doing slow stretching exercises on the floor — his movements as hypnotic and inevitable as waking after sleep, without, that is, a single superfluous twitch that might remove them from the purest beauty. He returned after each group to an erect, cross-legged posture with a delightful, small clicking of the joints. Before dinner, we would go for a walk across a deserted rail-track nearby or lie alongside Nilukaka on a small, oblong carpet, listening to stories he recounted of his regimental base:

'The jawans were expected to pass a rifle-shooting test before they could qualify for the next rank. The CO's wife called one morning to talk about her orderly. Captain, she said, you do know that Kartar Singh has to take time off from essential housework to do your tedious rifle-shooting test. Can I depend on you to see that he clears it? She was asking me to give him extra marks, and the fellow would have to fight a war one day. Were I

Biren-da, I'd have said, go to hell, ma'am, and keep Kartar Singh with you there. (Who else will dust the beds down in that place?) And left the good woman frothing at the mouth. So I said, ma'am, would you mind sending the fellow round for an hour of practice in the afternoons? I'll make sure your routine isn't disturbed. She couldn't very well refuse. Kartar Singh cleared the test with flying colours.'

A week later, I returned to school to laugh at the same small-mouthed nuns and groan over the hundredth gruel-dinner, yet it was all changed. The voices around me were flat, they seemed to come from frenzied puppets. At some point, I stopped listening altogether, and gave myself up to the grip of a low, moaning fever, wherein the face before me as I awoke each morning was Nilu's, the thoughts about him (if you can call a continuous reverber-ation thoughts) entering grimly into meals and bedtime, the games we played, and class. At prep, the lines on my book turned into a mildly vexing blur as I hung upon the beams of some recent incident involving the man: Was I lively enough the evening we went to the cinema? What exactly did he mean when he said I was somebody special? Frequently I would rouse myself to write to Bela a wordy, polysyllabic letter that I willed her brother to read, that he must surely read. I didn't speak much in those days and hardly ate, wandering about the premises, a tightrope-walking ghost.

Then the bubble burst. After the October tests, the Mother Superior entered Class Ten, swinging her rosary, her polished glasses gleaming more than usual, to distrib-ute reports. I made an attempt to dwindle away behind my desk, keeping my head down as Molly and Valdi, her two glistening, overfed dachshunds, frisked about my feet. The names of the girls at the top of the class were read out, Parminder Singh, Shalini Mehrotra ... then high marks in individual subjects. My name didn't figure. The Mother Superior stood still, looking intently at a small crucifix nestling in her palm:

'I'd like to share with all of you today my thoughts about one of your classmates, Megha. She's passed in everything, but where her marks used to be close to the highest, I see that they are worse than average now. Can it be that she's grown stupider in these last few months? That doesn't strike me as the likely answer. Have the lessons become more difficult suddenly? In that case,' she swooped, unfaltering, 'the rest of the class should have fared badly as well. The reason, I have a feeling,' said the sharp, black-eyed nun, turning to me, 'lies elsewhere. I want you to know that no mood or inattention on your part has escaped us ... Sister Maria thinks it may have to do with a visitor who calls on you each week.' I looked up, the wind gone out of my sails. 'I had hoped it wouldn't come to this, and you'd realize on your own that you can't burn your candle at both ends.'

She swept out grandly in rustling habit and crêpe soles, the dachshunds' nails clicking less jauntily beside her. I was gasping still. Did she think I was having an affair? It had the sound of depravity. What scenes of passion had the swarthy, pocked she-devil, Sister Maria, imagined for me in the hushed school parlour? I spent a sleepless night. Next morning, trembling with shame and anger, I confronted the Mother Superior as she emerged from morning Mass. She had, inappropriately for her punishing role, a name out of Shakespeare. Hermione.

'Why did you say I was burning out my candle?' I gabbled, distraught and reckless. 'Do you honestly believe I am having an affair? The man who comes to see me is an uncle, I touch his feet. He'd be very shocked. He's also leaving town within a week.'

She was silent at first, then said, very gently: 'You tell me, child, I want you to tell me.'

'On my honour,' I sputtered, tearful, 'I declare that I am not having an affair. I'm surprised that you can let Sister Maria's imagination influence you so. I think you're truly unjust.'

'But your marks,' wailed the nun. 'How do you explain those?'

'You watch out for next month's marks,' I rallied, in a trap, 'since that's all that counts with you. If they prove anything about me.'

'I'd like to believe you,' whispered Mother Hermione. 'You say that your next report will help ... it's all I ask. Go, wash your face now.'

Suddenly, I felt drained of the past weeks' fever as by an exquisitely keen hypodermic needle. Nilukaka, who remained cheerfully unaware of all the cloister-dramas he inspired, departed for his unit soon after. I spoke of him to Purry sometimes, softly, with satisfaction, but it was gone, the crazed wrapping of the day's routine round thoughts of him, his voice, the ineffable lope and stretch of his wicked limbs ... I was free once again to pursue the innumerable trivia that go to make a healthy childhood – in the eyes of nuns and other dour adults with lives not rifled through by romance.

In 1965, war broke out with Pakistan, which – since we got nowhere near newspapers or the radio – was as faintly unreal to us as every other concern of the teeming land (and city) outside. We prayed to God each night (though

41

the enemy was said to be wicked) to spare the lives of soldiers on both sides. There was black paper on the windows, yet prep continued with the old dull ferocity, with scant respect for the exigencies of war. As before, we exchanged egg shampoos and lavender talcum in the washrooms, dancing the Charleston after Sunday tea to a scratchy gramophone record. One day, Bela phoned. Her brother, who'd been fighting at Poonch on the western front, had been caught in the calf by an enemy bullet. His mother had rushed to the Amritsar hospital to which he'd been brought. Suddenly, in that moment, Nilukaka acquired a reality for me that he had never previously had, a contingent, perishable substance that joined him with the rest of us who were frequently sick and would – presumably – die one day.

In my last year of school, Bela went all secretive on me (her speech pitted with well-timed pauses) about her brother Nilu, a major of cavalry now. I discovered on probing that he wished to marry a Monica Mullick from Calcutta, the nineteen-year-old daughter of a wealthy gold merchant. I felt a pang that somebody should now have his whole attention, but – when all was said – he was an uncle, and thirteen years older than I. It also seemed right that of all my grim relatives, there should fall upon Nilu, a man of mysterious disappearances and connections, the quick, radiant net of a romance. Anything less would have dimmed the aura a bit. Monica, on the other hand, was not a Brahmin and Nilu's mother, Mami, a semi-lettered woman of unshakeable views, would not be brought round to discuss the alliance. If he is to choose the mother of his children, and no matter her sanskaras, why does he ask for my blessing? Certainly, he will not have it. Nilu wrote often to his mother in those days, pleading, giving her reasons to relent: when he lay wounded at the base hospital, it was Monica who had read to him, slaked his parched throat, offered him love in every way she knew. As each letter arrived, Mami entered the prayer room for longer spells, emerging with the muscles of her face rolled up into tight, white knots of obstinacy. Let her come to visit, she once said to Bela in the course of a family quarrel, but you can receive her. I won't stand under the same roof as that woman for a moment.

Then Nilu came down to quell his mother's fears and assure her of his loyalty, but it was no use. For some reason, he had asked Bela to keep his wedding plans secret from me, yet he came over to the convent one evening, ravaged, brown, his right arm in plaster. There had been a skiing accident at Gulmarg.

'Are you going to Calcutta from here?' I asked, wise and unable to resist it.

'Why Calcutta?' he said, going all cautious. 'Somebody's been talking to you.'

I played along. 'Calcutta for the sleek ladies and dancing at the Grand. Flury's cakes and the Trincas' crooner. That's what has you up there every year, is it not?'

He looked relieved. I joked about his brown face, holding his plastered wrist the while, I told him it would be all right. 'Yes,' he said, 'yes,' as if it really was the wrist that we were talking about. He looked tired and at the mercy of anybody who might choose to prod or ridicule him.

In December 1966, I did the Senior Cambridge examination, shedding tears over higher maths, and trotting off each morning (after genuflections to Saraswati and St Jude), my breast covered with good-luck charms. Nilu married Monica quietly the following January, and was disowned by his mother. I was holidaying with friends, and learned that he was visiting my parents, Ratna and Biren, as part of his honeymoon. What was it he really wanted, Monica's approval for the family or the other way round? One morning, as the grown-ups chatted over breakfast, my brother Sujit entered Nilu's bedroom and pulled out all his wife's expensive clothes from her suitcase, stamping on them, muddying some ... Ratna was heard to say that she felt Sujit was perhaps not receiving the attention he deserved.

CHAPTER FIVE

When Damyanti Misra walked up Katra market, thinking of the iron buckets at home, the ones with holes in them, the shops had just raised their shutters for the morning. She was, no matter what Beni Madho said, going to buy plastic ones. Easy to clean, they would be, and in such cheerful colours. Orange, red, it will be a sunrise every time you enter the bathroom, said the lodger upstairs when she had mentioned it. He was a handful, that one, making fun of people all the time. He had been with them two months, and already she caught herself telling him all sorts of things that she would never mention to Beni Madho or Urmila. She told him about the time she went off to a woman for lessons in English conversation. Why not, Ashwin had said, it's as good a language as any ... She would buy those buckets, put a shine into her day, thought Damyanti, then let Beni Madho ask why and for how much.

She walked past a sweetshop, a clock-maker, a general merchant selling plastic tablecloths with snakeskin patterns, combs and bottles with expensive ice-coloured fluids in them. Suddenly she heard it: cuckoo, a pause, cuckoo, another pause ... She retraced her steps to watch the bird go in and out of its pretty wooden home, the whirring chains and cobs. On an impulse, she climbed into the clock-maker's and stood pointing, out of breath, at the importunate bird.

'Not for sale,' squawked a spotty youth at the counter. 'It's here for repairs. Do you want to know the price of one?' he smirked. The wood, Damyanti noticed, had lost its gloss, the paint coming off in flecks from the surrounding leaves.

A young woman stood at the counter, also watching the cuckoo. She held out an arm with a gaily coloured wristwatch that the shopkeeper held as he peered into the dial. She's letting him touch her, thought Damyanti. The outstetched hand was as large as a man's, coffee brown, with the square fingernails painted a deep scarlet. The shopkeeper said something under his breath. The young woman laughed, flashing a great many white teeth through red lipstick and then emerged from the shop, blinking in the sun, as Damyanti herself came out of the door.

Damyanti noticed that a man selling guavas was looking sharp-eyed at her, then a tailor, who walked a certain distance, then turned and came back to take a closer look. The fruit vendor was grinning horribly through a battered cheek: 'Some people prefer the higher castes these days,' he said.

Damyanti crossed the road, running smack into Urmila, her friend, who eyed her like the rest, with a clear, culpable interest.

'What's the matter?' said Damyanti. 'Why is everybody staring like that?'

'What do you expect,' retorted Urmila, 'when you're walking practically arm in arm with her?'

'With whom? Oh, who is she? She didn't look quite . . . like you and me, I thought. Bold, asking men a lot of questions.'

46

'They all do, the young ones of today,' observed Urmila drily. 'There's little they want to hide about themselves either. That,' she said with emphasis, 'is Chandibai's daughter, Ujala. Chandibai had her taught to dance at a famous Benares gharana. The richest men here are now falling over each other to invite her to their homes.'

'Ram kaho, these depraved old men,' mused Damyanti. 'What can they want, chasing after such a young woman?'

Urmila looked at her in astonishment. 'Then you really don't know . . .' she slowly said.

'Know what?' asked Damyanti, but guessed before Urmila could reply. All those eyes, greedy with knowledge, ladling out humiliation for her like grit in the daal. The young woman was nearby still, examining some bright-coloured cotton prints on the pavement. Damyanti heard the clack of her thick pink-and-gold lacquer bangles from where she stood.

'Ujala,' said Urmila, unquenchable now, 'is Beni Madhoji's present . . . He's lost his mind, people say, and blubbers on her doorstep when she doesn't let him in. Beni Madhoji buys her clothes, takes her to the cinema. Neighbours hear them quarrelling sometimes. He'll break her leg, he says, if she goes to a rich man's house again . . . She does exactly as she pleases, of course, has him dancing on the palm of her hand.'

The young woman was weaving her way now slowly through the crowd.

'I have to go,' said Damyanti, thinking why did she have to tell me. 'The lodger upstairs has to be fed.'

She set off briskly, plastic buckets forgotten, following the young woman at about thirty paces. If she stopped, Damyanti stopped too, and looked at revoltingly coloured plastic merry-go-rounds that vendors held up to her. Ujala was tall and conquered the pavement with long strides.

47

She wore a blue nylon sari with arabesques in mauve and pink, and a perfectly cut blouse that held up high her proud, eager breasts. Her waist was that of a boy, and she swayed her hip lazily from side to side. At the end of a short walk, she climbed some steps and, entering a door, turned to face the bustling street.

There, below her, stood a timid woman with unironed clothes, the crow's feet round her eyes deepening with emotion. Damyanti. She looked into Ujala's face, numb before her glowing youth and jauntiness, her terrible audacity. Ujala had recently turned twenty-three. Her fingers played with a long chain bunched upon her breast as she looked at Damyanti with a black-eyed surprise (you aren't a man, she seemed to say, what can you want from this door), then turned on her heel and went indoors.

At home afterwards, Damyanti placed two aluminium pots with dented, black bellies on the fire, and walked to the room where she and Beni Madho slept. In the cupboard mirror, she saw a grim, wasted face above a heavy and useless body, with stains of turmeric on the sari. Her eyes, she felt, were torpid as a pariah dog's, asking, always asking, and with nothing to give. Beni Madho had once placed his palm flat against her stomach and wonderingly said, arid as a waterless well . . . Then she caught sight of her nose, the fine hopeful nose, perfect as a flute, her exquisite, pink ears. Before she knew it, they had welled up, heavy, reckless tears, coursing down her tightening cheek. Her head hurt. They said you had bad days and then you had good days, nothing was for ever. Except her life had never yet seen the morning . . . how long had one to keep it up?

'Mausi,' called a young voice, urgent across the court-

48

yard. It was Ashwin, the lodger, asking for his lunch, and there was none to give him.

'I was passing the kitchen,' he said in tones of having witnessed the apocalypse, 'and I smelt something burning. I think it's the rice . . . must have cleaved to the pot.'

She swiftly redeemed the cooked grain at the top with a large, flat spoon, and placed the cooking pot under a water tap. It hissed sharply, giving out a cloud.

'Have you been to the market?' asked Ashwin. 'I don't think lunch is ready . . . I can wait, but Misraji will be coming in soon.' Then he saw her red nose.

She washed and bleakly chopped some potatoes and parwal while Ashwin stood stirring the daal. He also washed some glasses lying in the sink. She was past caring, she let him.

'Misraji has a woman,' said Damyanti at last. 'A dancing girl, very young. I ran into her at the market today.'

Ashwin resumed stirring the daal.

'People say he's lost his mind over her,' ran Damyanti's voice, flat and unable to stop. 'Can't live without seeing the woman for a day. She's beautiful and arrogant.'

There was silence as Ashwin took the brass pitcher into the courtyard, and filled it with fresh water. When he returned, he absently lifted the pot of daal from the fire with his bare hands, and burned himself.

'Ufff,' he said, 'bloody fool.' Damyanti continued chopping her vegetable, wiping a leaky eye from time to time with her sari.

'I saw a play called *Hayavadan* recently,' said Ashwin, examining his fingers. 'There are two men in the story . . . one has a keen and agile brain, the other a marvellous, powerful body. A woman loves them both and finds that she is unable to choose between them. One day, the three

49

go off into the forest and come across the great goddess, Kali. They are overcome with emotion and want to offer sacrifice, so the two men cut off their heads and place them at the deity's feet ... Are you listening?'

'Yes,' said Damyanti, gently impatient. 'I'm listening.'

'The woman becomes distraught, flailing at the goddess, beating her breast till Kali takes pity and, with a laugh, restores the two men to life. But there's a difference. She places the good brain on the strong body, and the remaining halves together. Once again, the woman is asked to choose between them. She finds no difficulty this time, and goes away with the man of perfect endowment.'

'Is that all? Why are you telling me all this?' wailed the woman weakly.

'Shush, allow me a breath, will you? Years go by, and the clever, athletic man has all he wants – a home, love, social place, the admiration of his fellows. He ceases to strive in any area, neglecting to use both his brain and his muscle, and grows altogether complacent. One day, the woman notices that the man of her dreams has turned into a human cipher. And the other one? The feeble one, who was abandoned in the forest, struggles from one moment to the next, taxing his wits, straining his sinew, and acquiring a series of small talents. Just so he can survive without help, for he has no friends. He works for years without ceasing, but at the end of the pain and humiliation, the sweat and grittings of teeth, there he stands facing the world – a man with a masterful brain and perfect body, a conqueror.'

Damyanti sprinkled some heated oil with cumin and asafoetida. There was a hiss, an acrid smoke, and drops of oil stood on the wall behind the stove. 'I am the man,' she said, adding vegetable to the fiery effusion, 'who was left behind in the forest with a no-good brain and a no-good body.'

'Wrong,' tore Ashwin's voice, a hidden nail. 'You are the other one, who was given it all, but chose to lose it.' Through the sins of meddlesomeness and fidgeting, he touched the old blackened pot again, and burned himself a second time. 'Oooo oo,' he went, 'damned pot of daal,' and fled to hold his fingers under the tap.

Damyanti placed a bowl of ghee before him. 'Put that where it hurts,' she said. 'The skin won't blister, and the pain will go away.'

'You are the capable one who threw it all away,' persisted Ashwin, resolute on his course. 'You had a mind, but decided to put in camphor and seal it away, so Beni Madho could do your thinking for you. You could sing a decent thumri, but had the tongue cut out of your head. You could have gone out into the world, done some grand things, but you preferred to crouch here in this dark kitchen, a hump-backed dwarf. You even have a nice nose.'

At the mention of her nose, Damyanti began to cry again with childish snuffling sounds. She hid her eyes with her fingers.

'Achha mausi, bus mausi, I didn't mean to upset you, did I? And you're really long cooking that parwal. I'm famished.'

'What I mind most,' said Damyanti, swallowing, 'is my own worthlessness. Being nothing, a cipher ... I fear that one day I shall look into a mirror and find nobody there.'

'Back in Oxford,' said Ashwin after a pause, 'I have a girlfriend called Susan. Now she wouldn't have said what you just said.'

'You're all the same,' replied Damyanti. 'About women, you're alike, every one.'

'Alike? I wouldn't say that. I wouldn't go so far at all. When Susan had exams, for instance, I did the cooking, the cleaning of the house, washing up. At other times, we took turns.'

'You weren't married to this girl?'

'No.'

'Yet you lived under the same roof?'

'Yes,' said Ashwin, smiling a small smile. 'We did everything together. It was very nice.'

Damyanti averted her face. You couldn't speak to the young any more, they made you want to put your finger in your ear.

'C'mon, mausi,' he teased, enjoying her discomfort. 'It cut our expenses by half and made things so easy. Anyway, I was saying that if I were to leave Susan and go to another woman, she'd call me a crackpot. She'd say I didn't know how to keep a relationship. Susan wouldn't blame herself.'

'She's different,' replied Damyanti, failing to connect. 'She's a firangi.' Those laughing, yellow-haired women with pink, lined faces, what did they have to do with it?

Ashwin laughed, settling down to eat upon a white asana. 'Will Beni Madhoji's dancing girl last, do you think?' he asked.

She shook her head. 'There've been others ... school-teachers, once a nurse in a hospital. He's in a fever some months, then it wears off. This one is young, she'll go off with a rich man before long. Somewhere inside him, he's corrupt, Misraji, and it comes out in the end.'

'Yes,' said Ashwin, thoughtful now, 'but there will be other women. And this fever, as you call it, over and over again.'

They were silent as he ate his rice and dry vegetable. 'What you have to understand,' he went on with the insensitivity of the young, whose emotions still matched their ideals, 'is that Beni Madhoji goes to other women not because there's something the matter with you ... Hasn't it occurred to you that the man is too coarse either to grasp or to love something as gentle as you are? He goes from one woman to another because inside him, there's this ... this hole, an emptiness, and he's going to spend his entire life looking for something to fill it up with. Nothing will, it's almost as if he lacks a part, an organ, that the rest of us are born with. He's not destined for much happiness, is he, the poor man?'

'And I, what am I supposed to do?' asked a querulous Damyanti. 'Wait till he tires of squalid scenes with all his different painted women?'

Ashwin stopped eating. He looked up, suddenly sharp-eyed. 'That,' he said slowly, 'is a matter entirely of your choosing. Nobody can keep you from unhappiness if you're determined to make it your fate.'

It was easy for him to talk, educated, young, somebody who could walk out of any door he chose. Damyanti felt exasperated.

'I was asking myself the other night,' said Ashwin, 'why I work so hard at my job. Hours in the library, making notes up to three o'clock in the morning. One, I decided, because I want to hold my head up before everybody. Once I manage that, it won't matter what my father or my students, even Susan, think about me. Not much, at any rate. The good feeling has to come from in there,' he said, a little dramatically, touching his breast with an index finger.

Suddenly, he felt ashamed. There he was, talking to a poor, believing woman in distress over her worthless husband as if she was one of his students. Ashwin tried to put the feeling away.

'Do me a favour,' he said, without emphasis, 'put your own eyes on instead of those duds, and go take a look at the world. Say to Beni Madho, here are your eyes, they've come in handy many years, but thanks, you can have them now. Talk to people, see how they live, and you'll discover a most surprising thing: Beni Madho did not create the world. Somebody did, and if you try very hard, maybe you'll even find out *how* one day. With what materials . . .'

'And this house, how do I live here?' said Damyanti, whining still but taken, distinctly taken, with the heady words.

'You could pull out your taanpura from its awful, dusty nest above my room for a start, and get it tuned. Then, perhaps you could polish up that singing voice of yours?'

'How did you know I sang?' she said, nervous but pleased.

'I'm a spy,' replied Ashwin. 'I've heard you try out all sorts of things when you thought nobody was in the house. Without training, nobody could possibly take those whirling taans you do. Your voice, lady, still has range.'

'The things he says,' muttered Damyanti. 'I'll have to become another person.'

'Then do that, for the love of God, do it.' He had finished washing his hands. 'You know what you'll have to start with? Get rid of that awful palla from your hair. What's it for, anyway?'

'Ram, this boy is crazy. Married women don't leave their heads uncovered.'

'Is that all you are, married?' asked Ashwin, banging a steel glass with impatience. 'Isn't there anybody inside those clothes, that mangalsutra? Let's see her. And when you talk, look up – like this – into my eyes. You've got nothing to hide ... Look, for heaven's sake, at a man's face when you address him.'

Damyanti thought of what Urmila would say if she saw her with her palla down, laughing and talking to people. She felt amused, the same as when Beni Madho had acted in a play, dressed up as a woman. She remembered the false hair hanging low upon his brow, a sari and high, pointed breasts.

'Last of all,' said Ashwin, carefully watching her glinting eyes, the upward curve of her mouth, 'I shall buy you a skirt. You'll wear it and walk down Civil Lines, arm in arm with me. They'll wonder where I found you.'

'Go away,' said Damyanti. 'You've finished lunch long ago. And wasted my entire afternoon, talking rubbish.'

'I have, haven't I?' he said. 'Why, you can't wait to hear the voice of God again. Here he comes now, chugging like a steam engine.' Beni Madho crossed the courtyard, grimacing, mopping his brow.

A rude young man, she thought. Why does he live in our poor lodgings, no fridge, no sitting room, when he can clearly afford better? Is he what he called himself then, a spy? Working for a foreign country ... or the police? What can he expect to find in our home, except Beni Madho's trashy memories? One has to be careful, she said to herself, he has a way of making one talk more than is seemly or wise.

CHAPTER SIX

After a lazy Vividh Bharati and Perry Mason-filled winter in the sun, I was sent to a private college in Lucknow for undergraduate studies. There, incarcerated once again behind the beautiful red brick of a convent, I failed to discover any facts of importance about the city I lived in, its preoccupations and prejudices. The nuns who ran the college were Irish, which is to say they were witty, irreverent, romantic and visited with sudden bouts of craziness. They drew us into an oasis of pleasure-filled reading, where we grew to scorn (with a naivety that would endure) venal ambition, conformity and pettiness. In my case, they dredged up all the aberrations of my childhood (the intensity and loneliness and fear), determined to transform them into a gift, a talent for something ... They left me as their only discourtesy an impatience with the commonplace, men talking shares, pay packets or promotions, and women their mothers-in-law: I cannot accept that life has at any moment the right to be dull.

Within the college, there were few rules, and to those freshers with pasts of a crippling restraint, the freedom came as a heady draught. They took to visiting Hazratgunj, the shopping area, astride creaking rickshaws, wearing crêpe and chiffon, eye-shadow and towering coiffures.

Everyone, including those of us in faded skirts and sneakers, was gated after the first fortnight. Stop this peacock-like preening at once, said Mother Bernardine in dismay, for each batch of freshers would bring its own brand of over-reaction to the first swigs of independence, along with innocence, a rebellion against authority, and a fund of misconceptions about what life really had to offer. Two years later, an unremarked day scholar called Saira Munim would be chosen as Miss India in the Femina contest, and quietly asked to leave the college. I won't have my girls aiming to be beauty queens, Mother Bernardine would say at grace before dinner, staring thoughtfully at her swollen, pink toes. We bring you up to be serious people who, from the store of things they think and learn to feel on these premises, will one day make a contribution to their country, maybe even to the world. Afterwards, in the common room, we would sing: 'Let's murder Berda, yeah-yeah-yeah, why don't you and us combine / Let's murder Berda right away, we can have a swingin' time.' Yet, distended still with dreams of achievement that were laughably larger than life, secretly, in our hearts, we approved the gesture.

The Germans who taught me at school had pointed to mathematics and science (with furrowed mouths) as the right provender for growing minds. Poetry was mainly for the wallowings of lesser brains. I believed them. Till in college, the small Zenobia Mistry, who, with her shining black curls and looking scarcely older than us, climbed up and sat on the teaching desk. Her eyes were a warm brown and, without an introduction, she began to intone in a voice that was the texture of honey slowly stirred in butter:

> 'Others because you did not keep
> That deep-sworn vow

57

Have been friends of mine.
Yet always when I look death in the face,
When I clamber to the heights of sleep
Or when I grow excited with wine,
Suddenly I meet your face.'

In the next class it was 'Tintern Abbey', then Robert Graves, and back again to 'Ode on a Grecian Urn', in what seemed a terrible confusion of choice. Gradually, the teacher conjured mountains in the night, where the spirit shudders and becomes still, firelight or the ashen dawn that follows the loss of love. She gave us images to free associate with, unleashing for our dim brains a spectrum of emotion, uxoriousness—guilt—pity—desperation. Sensations we merely guessed at in those years, but neither recognized nor could successfully name. Allen Tate had taught her in an American university, and Robert Frost had come to address her class. She spoke of love, and on her bony, brown hand glittered a ring with many diamonds: there was a fiancé back in Minnesota, Herb something. One day, in the middle of a Yeats poem, a diamond fell out and rolled away beneath the rows of desks. We looked everywhere. In the weeks that followed, Miss Mistry turned up in class with puffy eyelids and a tired smile. The engagement with Herb had come to an end.

Which was about the time when Zenobia and I first became friends. She laughed at most things, but in class Zenobia transformed learning into a deep everyday pleasure, linking the subject-matter of a hundred dusty books with the keen—agonizing—intractable business of living for us. She lent her books freely, so I filled my days with William Golding and Graham Greene, Hemingway, Bernard Malamud and all English poetry in the lyrical mode, with never a thought for the syllabus.

Zenobia had a friend, Priti Singh, who taught European history. She was stylish, a little burned away at the edges, and desperately in search of some immutable to which she could wholeheartedly give her allegiance. Most of the time, she was passionately in love with somebody, with an emotion just this side of idolatry. She led me to *The Alexandria Quartet*, Gide and Cocteau, and to a taste for certain periods of European painting, the Renaissance, the post-Impressionists. We talked for hours, Zenobia, Priti and I, revealing our most secret motives, laughing without restraint at each other, and subtly, without the least intent, the two women shaped in me a taste for, and a lifelong commitment to, beauty as the final value. Was it wrong? Is anything good ugly? I shall never know. I learned only in later years of the pain, the scarring pain, that had to accompany the pursuit of loveliness. And the toll it took in imperceptible ways upon what was (in most of our cases) a tenuous sanity.

In the first year, 'lights out' in the dormitory was at eleven o'clock. So if I had some reading to finish, I would retreat to the washrooms at the end of the sleeping cubicles, and curl up for an hour or so on the floor. One night, I found a tall girl in plaits and glasses leaning against a washbasin, and quietly filing her nails. One didn't speak to seniors unless introduced, so I got on with reading Durrell's *Antrobus*, laughing aloud to myself several times. Binna Shourie, for that was her name, looked sternly a few times over her spectacles at this vibrating huddle, but said nothing. The following night, she came in again, to wash her face or the sleep out of her eyes. Without the glasses, her eyes looked distracted, far away, the skin around them pale. She always wore a red skirt and a loose white blouse.

'You seem to be here every night,' she said, yawning and without emphasis. 'Don't you find it difficult to wake up in the mornings?'

'I don't try,' I replied. 'I normally sleep through break-fast and the first class.'

She smiled. 'The night is certainly a better time for doing some things. And sometimes, because you can't see too clearly, your other senses get sharpened ... Have you ever tried being out at this hour?'

'But the building is locked,' I protested, defending my failure, 'and a chowkidar, however drugged and decrepit, sits outside the door.'

'There are exits and exits,' replied Binna. 'Some just lead out. I'm talking of paths which, if you can find them, bring you smack up amidst the stars. Take the roof of this building. Have you seen it yet?'

We were on the top floor, with no stairs in sight that could lead us out of the block. We first dropped over a wall to a lower terrace, then with the aid of several dark pipes and small ledges, footholds that sometimes gave beneath our feet, we climbed through blackness and drying moss to a burst of open space, and the warm, lapping sky was about us. Every night afterwards, when our reading was done, we emerged upon the terrace, breathless from the fear and the pleasure, with mats, an alarm clock, sheets, sometimes even a packet of daalmoth. We paced the roof, talking about the books and people we knew, and the kind of persons, pompous—phony—avaricious, we had to make sure we didn't become in the years to come.

'What d'you want to do after you leave college?' asked Binna once, in the direct, unembarrassed way she had, investing the person before her with a sudden significance.

I hadn't a clue. I just knew it wasn't going to be parties

or small talk, or a life of daily drudgery. 'I think I'll be a judge,' I said, 'and change the popular belief that women can make only emotional decisions.' (I was still too stupid to suspect the importance, the heartrending importance, of emotion in the scheme of things, how it made an act vibrant or human, how it engendered – in the final call – morality.) 'Whatever it is, Binna,' I said with the idiocy of my years, 'it will have to have a clear intellectual dimension, a life of the mind.' Which didn't leave me with too many profes- sions to choose from. 'And who will you be?'

'I've been thinking,' replied Binna slowly, making a vault with long, skeletal fingers. 'I want to do something that involves people, helping them. If I read psychology, I can become a counsellor who talks people out of killing themselves, wrecking their marriages, that sort of thing. There's a great deal I have to learn, undergoing therapy myself, to begin with, to straighten out the knots.'

'Do you really believe we can help other people solve life's perplexing riddles? Does any one person have all the answers? I think each of us has to muddle her way through the tricky and painful situations and, if we're both patient and lucky, hit upon a solution ourselves sometimes. For the rest, the problem itself passes,' I sagely added. 'Rem- edies given by others are never quite the thing, are they? The truth lies somewhere inside us.'

Binna wiped her glasses. 'Possibly,' she murmured, 'but when things are going wrong, our minds too stop giving the answers they otherwise might. It's one of the character- istics of a truly bad time: you feel you're in a corner, a dead end. That's where a counsellor comes in, somebody who looks at the situation dispassionately, with no real stakes in your life. It must be nice to have the support of a person stronger than you, in front of whom you can shamelessly collapse ... These days we have problems with my brother at home. Nothing awful, and I don't really want to discuss it ... but on the days I feel disturbed, you help me quite a lot, you know?'

'I!' said I, incredulous. 'That's the first I'm hearing of it. We meet at night for a couple of hours and giggle over the girls cramming for exams, or at teachers pretending to wisdom where they lack even the rudiments of their own discipline. How do I help?'

'That's how,' she replied. 'By being who you are. When I'm with you, I don't have to run so hard, or struggle, or pretend about the things I feel. You speak from your innermost thoughts and lack a sort of top skin. Please just stay that way, honest and funny.'

We finally tired of pacing the moss-blacked terrace, and lay down on chatais, covered all round by a marquee of cool and tiny stars. It was heaven, and we fell asleep, listening to the rustle of mango and eucalyptus, to the last whirrs and frets of the city that was being snuffed out against its will about us. At four o'clock, in the dark, the alarm went off and we climbed down to our hot cubicles in sleepy disgust, I to more sweaty sleep, and Binna to reading psychology to an early sunrise. She would go after graduation to an American university, and spend many years seeking the truth about existence in the land of therapists and hamburger steaks and Steven Spielberg.

The roof episode came to a slightly tedious end one night when Binna was caught by Mother Bernardine, completing a perfect billowy leap to a lower terrace. We were both gated for the rest of the term. When I asked the nun why, 'Lord love me,' she said, 'I can't have fifty-six lasses climbing that path to the roof. It makes my stomach turn just thinking about it. One or the other would surely break her neck.'

So I read Adler and Rousseau and the Bhagavad Gita,

missing classes, sleeping through the mornings, while Binna played tennis, practised on the piano, and read psychology, English and economics till she was ready to drop. We have to learn so much in a day, she would say, that we never go to bed the same people as woke up in the morning. Inside our heads, we will grow an inch each day ... Our room-mates put up pictures of Michael Caine and Alain Delon on the walls: Binna and I were happy so long as they allowed Alan Bates and Kabir Bedi playing Tughlaq to hang beside them. Sometimes, we stole the chowkidar's bicycle to ride into town at a forbidden hour and snatch a quick hamburger and Coke, but it was the theatre which got Binna and me in the end.

Before I joined college, Binna had been around, playing a Tony Lumpkin or Feste for the annual plays. Mother Bernardine, who had studied theatrical direction at Trinity College, Dublin, watched me for several months after I arrived (is her face too regular, her voice too deep?), then cast me as a thirteen-year-old, Anne Frank, in a three-act tearjerker of her choice. (Every play we seemed to choose at college just heaved and gagged with emotion; it was also perhaps the reason why each was a great commercial success in the city.) Binna played the boyfriend, Peter Van Daan. I skulked around the corridors for weeks before the performance, dazed and despairing by turns, clutching at small hopes, inhabiting all day (in my head) the stifling attic that Anne Frank lived in with her family. On the night of the dress rehearsal, we had two critics from Hollywood, one an actress, Diane Baker, who came up afterwards and gave generous praise. To me, she said: 'When it comes to the climax of a scene, resist the urge to understate. Let the occasion fan out and swell. Let yourself swell. You have to take your moment.'

The play did well, and was widely reviewed. In the

years that followed, there were other plays, long and short, in which I played Viola or Candida or Jane Seymour, with Binna cast opposite me as Eugene or Henry VIII. The rehearsals took up all our evenings, there was consider-able applause for the performances and, in us, a sort of drunkenness. The relationship between Binna and me often took its curve from the characters we were playing at the time, derision or great love or a naked hostility. If we played brother and sister, our talk outside rehearsals took the form of merciless teasing. Yet when I was Jane Sey-mour and Binna Henry, we could scarcely bear to sit at the same table for dinner, passing dishes, only if asked, in a bristling, angry silence. It was something neither of us understood, this domination by the people we pretended to be, this being worked by strings ... We talked a lot less, but still took time off to tip snatches of our daily reading into each other's lockers. Binna's notes read:

The mind is most concrete not when it inspects, as an observer, but when it passionately cares about what is before it. If we seek reality, we shall find it in experience deeply and anxiously felt.

E. J. Hocking

or

... there is no god apart from poppies and the flying fish, men singing songs, and women brushing their hair in the sun. The lovely things are god that come to pass.

D. H. Lawrence

The world, it seemed, had just come into being, with us the first plunderers of its rich, wild fruit.

CHAPTER SEVEN

For my eighteenth birthday, Priti and Zenobia arrived after dark in a Fiat car, into which Binna and I were eagerly bundled and whisked away under the chowkidar's nose for an evening of quiet celebration. We soon drove past a museum, a canal, two railway stations, and beyond the dusty, ill-lit edges of the city to Priti's beautiful home on a farm, where she lived with her parents in a peevish silence in return for past persecutions, real and imaginary, and the unexamined luxury and elegance they now offered. The parents were out when we arrived, so in lamplight, to the sound of a horn concerto by Bach, I was given my first gin. The sofas we sat on were covered with a dull-emerald tapestry, Zenobia wore Diorissimo, a faint floral perfume, and there was grapefruit for starters ... It wasn't the evening's conversation (for none of it remains) or eating wild duck, or even the log fire that burned briskly at the tiny living room's edge that made the evening memorable, but what it revealed about the gathered company. For at least two of us (Priti and I) would always remain in some measure what we were on that evening, greedy for sensation, grateful for the scraps of elegance and new knowledge that fell our way, and continually in search of such people as would intensify our moments of experience, and throw them into the sharpest relief.

That summer we met again in Nainital, going for walks, lounging about the Boathouse Club in the afternoons, and being rowed by a new and athletic Priti several times across the lake. My parents, with whom I was staying at the Waldorf, made a huge fuss about the hours I was spending with my teachers. Somewhere, suspected my father, I was growing up a lot faster, in more complicated ways, than his plans for me had room for. I met Binna and the teachers in the churchyard of St John in the Wilderness one afternoon, with just the woods about us, warming ourselves in the skittish sunlight that teased the silent grass. We had a lunch hamper, and Zenobia lay on a rough stone wall, reading out from Keats:

> 'Then glut thy sorrow on a morning rose,
> Or on the rainbow of the salt sand-wave.'

Her voice had about it the rustling on-and-on quality of the wind and trees about us that afternoon. Priti took a lot of photographs, turning my poor flinching face this way and that, attributing to me a handsomeness at that age which, with my boniness and knitted brows, my dull clothes, and the sudden silences of my everyday speech, I could not by any stretch have possessed.

> 'Or if thy mistress some rich anger shows,
> Emprison her soft hand and let her rave,
> And feed deep, deep upon her peerless eyes.'

That night, we had dinner at the Metropole, where my friends were staying, and sat afterwards, looking down at

Nainital from behind the long, white pillars of a verandah. Every so often, a cloud would sweep up, fleecy, damp, blocking the township from view, yet each time we readied ourselves for blankness and night, Nainital would spring up again, virgin and glittering in the downy dark, reluctant to let us go. We sat on white cane chairs, drinking Drambuie.

'Take the smallest drop,' said Priti, ever the pedagogue, ever in her element, 'and roll it on your tongue, like this. And see what it does to your eyes and face and brain.' Reverently we sipped, Binna and I, and were – with an answering credulity – warmed to the cockles. I sang a Hindi song of the 'fifties, about belonging to somebody till after the moon and stars were erased.

'How d'you like Erich Fromm?' asked Zenobia, embarrassed, and a little uncertain about the nature of Priti's influence upon us. I had borrowed her copy of *The Art of Loving*.

'I've a few pages to go still, but it's good,' I replied. 'It's excellent.' In a moment the Drambuie would dredge up my callowness, strip it bare. 'What beats me is why an obviously remarkable man would write a whole book on that subject. Love. Is love so central to everybody's life? Does it always wield such power? I feel that most people get by quite nicely without it, then along comes some daydreamer who runs headfirst into the grand emotion – wham – emerging at the other end pulped, mangled, a mouse caught in a sugarcane press.'

'Don't sound stupider than you must,' reproved Zenobia. 'There are so many kinds of love. Haven't you heard of young children who miss out on human warmth altogether? They turn autistic, unable to reach out to others or fend for themselves, unable even to survive.'

'But they don't die, do they,' I persisted, 'except from

67

dire bodily want. Or exposure. I put it to you that of the people we meet in our daily lives, only a very few have encountered actual feelings of love. In themselves or in others.'

'What's all this?' said Priti, extricating herself from an impromptu lecture to Binna on the historical place of Hindi films of the 'fifties. Pop art conveying the finest local values. Binna, who felt that Indian cinema of the period copied shamelessly from Charlie Chaplin, ragtime and western saloon bars, was stifling a yawn. 'I believe I hear a row in progress,' continued Priti. 'Tell me about this book, somebody. Has to be a cracker to set off such a burning in our literature-wallahs' breasts. Has it a central idea?'

'Sure it does,' leaped Binna, who had stolen my copy to read during economics class. 'And don't interrupt, Megha. The book proposes that love is not a happening, a catastrophe, to which people are helplessly subject, but a process, a creative process, in which you play "giver" by choice. Fromm describes love as an organism that we make and renew. A matter of continuous doing.'

'Sounds a bit laboured,' remarked Priti, turning to Zenobia for confirmation. 'The way I look at it, it either happens to you or it doesn't, and not everybody's lucky.'

Zenobia frowned. As always, Priti was going too fast, judging what she did not yet comprehend. 'You have to read Fromm, Priti, the man's a first-rate analyst of the neo-Freudian school. He defines love as a fully adult act, in which a human being is called upon to demonstrate what depths of experience, what responsibility, he is capable of taking on. Whether he can rise to a certain, I regret the word, nobility.'

Strains of a dance number from *Teesri Manzil* could be heard indoors, its guitars and cymbals gone wild. Binna and I rose on cue and began to shake different parts of our anatomy in the manner of Shammi Kapoor, jelly-like, with eyes starting, and hair flying into our faces. As suddenly, the din ended, and in its place came the unmistakable clunk of a lone forefinger trying out a minuet on a grand piano. With an equal readiness, Binna and I flattened our skirts and glided into a mincing pas-de-deux, our faces composed into masks, but the forefinger went on and on, so in a while, we bowed to each other deeply, exaggeratedly, and sat down again.

There was more Drambuie, darkness where we sat, and Binna resumed: 'One hears so often of a memorable love followed by a loss, a parting of ways with the loved one. Would you say in that circumstance that the love was still worth having had?'

Priti was watching Zenobia, who thought of leaves — gold, rust and orange — in the Minnesota fall, and Herb kissing her frozen lips in a pale, pre-winter moonlight.

'A great loss,' said Zenobia, tonelessly, 'can fragment the personality, warp your brain, and take away all kindness from you.'

We sat in silence, letting the dense draught of Zenobia's pain seep down our quickened senses. 'Yet if you've loved once,' spoke the daft, lovable Binna in a while again, 'I wonder whether you can ever be truly petty or venal again. Doesn't the experience sort of raise you above the plunder-ing herd, bring you to a new order of things?'

The teachers laughed aloud; where was the experience that made you permanently anything? There was nothing you didn't forget (promises as children, family pride). Nothing whose memory you did not defile one day with some trivial and nasty act in the name of everyday survival. Or did you?

'I can't see anything changing you,' I said to pip

Binna's grand-naive mood, the secret expectation from life it revealed.

'I just know,' said Priti, unexpectedly then, 'that it's a very deep impulse, maddening, breaking all bounds, even the fear of making oneself ridiculous. There's nothing paticularly moral about love either. It comes upon its object with the brute pounce of a carnivore, leaving either party little choice, intent only upon the satisfaction of its appetite. You're helpless,' ended Priti Singh, who would always love ardently and, when the fever faded, always abandon the loved one with a shrug, a dry kiss, the little rationalization.

I graduated the following year with a tired second-class degree. Biren, who sat in a car beside the chauffeur, was reading my results out of a newspaper: 'I wouldn't have minded,' he said very softly, 'if you'd been an out-and-out failure . . . got a third. There's something even interesting about that. What bothers me is that my child should be mediocre. I loathe mediocrity.'

CHAPTER EIGHT

About seven thirty in the evening, Ashwin Krishna came running down, two steps at a time, late for an appointment with his friend Udai Bir Singh of the history department. They were to meet at the Prayag railway station so they could stand about like overgrown schoolboys, which they weren't, or social historians, which they proposed to be, watching the local life. He slowed down as he saw Damyanti folding clothes in the court-yard, raising his hand in a salute. She pretended not to notice, so he raced on, thinking, silly woman, now that she's spilt the beans on Misra, she'll probably go around sulking for days. Perhaps I should let her believe that her speaking out was my fault. Was it? Damyanti thought, in fact: the fellow's been out God knows where all night. He's twenty-seven years old, nor am I his mother, why should I worry? The trouble is, he hasn't touched any food . . . just been sleeping the whole blessed day.

The previous night, Ashwin Krishna had gone for dinner to Udai Singh's house, where the latter lived with parents, grandparents, a wife and a few aunts and uncles. Very impressive it had been, the drive up from the gates, breaking through a tangle of unswept undergrowth till they were met at the end by four white-clad servants in bandhini turbans, who walked alongside the car to the house. Udai's father, clearly the patriarch, had been resplendent in a traditional angarakha and fleecy white moustache. He spoke little, but when he embraced Ashwin, hugely, with warmth, the latter felt a sneaking guilt that, for him, the thakur would always be a relic, picturesque, strong, but failing somewhere in 'reality'. On the other hand, with his serfs and bondsmen down in Mewar, he must have been a tyrant, levying tithes, watching beatings administered . . . one never really knew. The men of the house gathered for dinner, and were served partridge and rice with saffron out of real silver. A silent meal aside from sounds of mastication, with Ashwin wondering what Udai's wife was like. It was unlikely that he would meet her since the women kept separate quarters. Did Udai himself meet her stealthily in the night, slipping in by a side door? After listening to some Kesarbai 78s in Udai's rooms, Ashwin began to feel the need for air. The windows of the house, if beautifully carved, were small and tightly shut. They drove first aimlessly around the sleeping city in Udai's new ambassador, Chatham Lines, Poonappa road, Civil Lines, then – as the idea grabbed both of them simultaneously – headed for the Ganga.

They talked desultorily of Udai's favourite period, Mughal India, and civic planning in Akbar and Sher Shah Suri's times, the peerless durbar buildings of the later Mughals, their advanced social etiquette, till around two in the night, they came to sit upon the moonless sands, and hear the lap and glide of the gentle river. From two lighted canopies in the distance came the sound of harmoniums and recitation in praise of the goddess Durga, a Bhagvati Jagaran. Ashwin lay back on the warm sand, letting his mind go still under a sky with a million burning points. He hadn't seen so many stars since he was a child, and no sodium lamps obtruded yet to pink the cool black of the holy city to unnatural wakefulness.

'Did you tell your wife not to wait up?' he asked Udai conversationally, in a while. 'She might stay awake and worry.'

'Somebody will tell her,' said Udai, dismissively. 'Probably a manservant.'

Ashwin looked at Udai's impassive face in disbelief. When you got used to it, you could even see expressions in the dark. Was Udai one of those peculiar men who married to beget children, and thought no more of their wives between the acts of engendering? 'Is your wife educated?' asked Ashwin Krishna with his natural impro-priety, eager to get to the bottom of this.

'Remarkably well,' answered Udai, turning to him in surprise. 'She's very accomplished, designs silver jewellery, little bowls and plates, that sort of thing.'

'But she doesn't like to meet your friends, is that it? Or their wives?'

'She does,' replied Udai, his patience beginning to wear thin. 'It's that the little one, our son, takes up all her time. She likes to go to bed when he does, around nine o'clock.'

So he had a son. 'Maybe it's something the West does to you, but I find it unfair,' said Ashwin, 'that you and I should lie here, under the stars, while a slave stays home and worries about nappies and early-morning feeds.'

'You don't give up, do you?' returned Udai quietly. 'I could be a little tired of the subject. In fact, I'm sick to death already.' They were silent for a while, then slowly, resentfully, Udai spoke: 'If you must know, she'll be on the phone right now, talking to her lover in Bombay.'

'No,' said Ashwin. 'C'mon, just because you're out one night, you don't have to start imagining things.'

73

'Whether I'm in or out, at twelve o'clock sharp, this bloke calls up every night. I'm often asleep and want to wring his neck when the phone rings, but she just says "Excuse me," all polite, and goes into the other room to talk to him. It's a businessman who works between Bombay and Hong Kong.'

'Sounds awful,' said Ashwin. 'But why should it happen ... to you, I mean? Have you spoken to her about it? Strongly, I mean. It's what we leave unsaid that often makes the trouble.'

Udai lit a cigarette. 'I've tried everything, scenes, appealing to her sense of honour, even threats of murder – that was when I still loved her. She says it's a childhood sweetheart whom her father wouldn't let her marry. Now we've come to a sort of truce: everything goes just so long as we never have to speak to each other.'

Ashwin was aghast: 'But it's your wife, damn you, not somebody else's worthless son we're speaking of. She lives in your house, brings up your child ... Don't you feel people owe *you* something?'

Udai turned to him with a weariness that belonged more to ageing fathers than to young husbands who were just starting life. Do they, he seemed to say. Aloud, he said: 'Actually, she's a nice girl ... I can see that she can't help herself. That chap has come to stand for all the things she saw in her own father, perhaps wanted to be herself.'

Ashwin had an urge to hit him, savage the fellow. 'Fuck other people's wants,' he said. 'What is it that you need? Wouldn't you like a woman who's looking for something *you* have to offer?'

'Yes,' said Udai, 'maybe. But I can't leave a woman in the lurch, can I? That rogue won't marry her, he's got a rich wife himself.'

If it would have helped to bang his own head on something, Ashwin would readily have grabbed the nearest boat's prow. Bloody Indians, he thought with frustration, they'll let anybody walk all over them, just so long as they can reveal some fine, useless motive like honour or chivalry deep down inside. So long as they have to *do* bloody nothing ... Damyanti Misra faces up to her emotion, at least, she's even able to express her sense of loss. He thought of how he had first come to Allahabad, an unconnected ghost with a few ideas, living on the borders of Indian existence, until she — with the extreme confidence of her demands, her vivid lower-middle-class candour — had drawn him into the thick undergrowth of the city's life. He felt a gratitude, as if he owed Damyanti his existence in some manner. Turning to Udai, he said:

'Yet it must rankle, touch a raw nerve, each time one contemplates the treachery of a near one?'

Udai looked at him as if he was an idiot, with anger. 'It does,' he replied, under his breath. The humiliation. 'I have often thought of drowning myself.'

The sky had lost its stars in the east, and was lightening, as they watched, to a pale blue-grey wash. Crows, the first birds up that morning, rose silently in twos and threes to fly to positions of vantage. There would soon be flowers and coconut and sweets made from milk offered to the holy waters. Already, a thin straggle of bathers was in sight, walking down a slope to the water. Then the temple bells began, the big, the medium and the small, with their heavy-bellied, euphonic call across the sands, and temple priests on their morning aarti, singing 'Om Jai Jagdish Hare'.

As a hesitant sun bobbed gently out of the grey, swaying Ganga, Ashwin saw his companion glare at a fat priest reaching out to stroke a young girl's fearful shoulder, and there was life waiting round the corner, pulsing, free, a shock to the senses each time. Udai and he threw off their clothes, and at a distance from the by-now manically prodding and gesticulating priests and some fervent housewives, plunged into the cold water to race each other to a little boat that was moving sleepily upstream. Once, as Udai fell behind, Ashwin turned around to check whether the fellow might in fact be trying to drown himself. Then Udai came up and grabbed his ankle and, in a moment, shot past a cursing Ashwin to the boat ahead. They sat afterwards before a shop, eating hot jalebis with tea, and Ashwin asked the shopkeeper for bhang, a little ball of marijuana. The man looked suspiciously at him first, was he a policeman, then seeing Ashwin's long hair, sent a boy racing to a nearby paan shop for the stuff. They ate many more jalebis after the bhang, and around nine Udai dropped Ashwin home.

'See you at Prayag station, sevenish,' said Udai. 'You'll see more of what the locals do, you bookish bastard.'

As he entered the Prayag railway station, Ashwin saw Udai's pistachio-green ambassador roll softly into the parking lot ... maybe he'd had a chat with his wife after all. Though, knowing Udai's talent for evasion, the chat would not have got him very far. In twos and threes, students from the university hostels were strolling or sitting on benches, or examining train times on a lighted board. You could tell the boys from A. N. Jha by their inconspicuous white and grey shirts and trousers, the English words in their speech, and a slight embarrassment at being caught doing what the locals did, drinking chai at Prayag. The boys from G. N. Jha and the other hostels were more in charge, with blue-and-yellow patterns on their shirts and loud laughter when a young woman with a mousy, brown plait walked quickly, nervously past them, her eyes on her painted toenails. Some held hands, even embraced each other, as she went. As the lights of the station brightened and the microphones crisply announced that the Kalka was ten minutes late, Ashwin saw the young woman drop her slippers, nervously still, and climb a red weighing machine that whirred and flashed with lights, cranking out its little reward with the smudged face of a film star on one side.

He drank tea with Udai, who was telling the tea stall owner about Ashwin's Ph.D. from England, that he wasn't yet married ... Suddenly, he grabbed a startled Ashwin's hand and held it, palm up, for Haldi Ram, the students' favourite palmist, to read. It was the last thing Ashwin wanted, somebody telling his fortune, with the solemnity such humbug inspired in this country, but he wasn't going to offend the chai wallah.

'Two more teas,' Haldi Ram ordered his assistant, they would be on the house. He soon alternated between kneading and peering into Ashwin's long, dry hand and holding a very dirty duster to his thoughtful upper lip. Then he spoke: 'This babuji's Ph.D. is what my matric was for me, the Sri Ganesh or starting point of his life. He will always study, and write many books.'

'What about?' muttered Udai. 'The sex life of the Allahabadi?'

'No,' said Haldi Ram, offended. 'About those of our customs which reveal the history of this land. He will write about politics, too. I'm puzzled,' he said, searching Ashwin's face. 'You're here throwing ice water on people, shaking them out of their quiet habits. You'll even change some lives ... but tell me, babuji, can a man caught in an earthquake himself give others shelter?'

77

'Earthquake, what earthquake?' demanded Ashwin, irritably.

'A brief and very painful one,' replied the tea-seller. 'I see a letter.' He was halted by a deafening whistle, followed by the mad trample of several hundred people, passengers with tin trunks, coolies in scarlet with brass plates on their arm, ticket checkers in caps and black jackets, who materialized from some dingy inner rooms and swarmed on to the platform. People pushed after a coolie, and could be seen minutes later running with the same urgent belief, after the same coolie, in the opposite direction. Soon the Kalka arrived, a dark and hurling giant, jetting smoke through its nostrils, the booming wheels and pistons going in a marvellous charged rhythm. The smell of coal dust mingling with faeces was everywhere. Bedrolls and baskets choking with mango or guava began to be hauled by porters and cursing men into second- and third-class compartments. Haldi Ram, who saw the train every day, rasped inaudibly for a few moments longer and stood afterwards, completely forgotten.

As the train left, the two lecturers walked up the emptying platform to four silent students in blue-and-yellow patterned shirts, staring listlessly at a straggle of low shanties across the tracks. Udai recognized one of them from his class, and Ashwin quickly grabbed Udai's cigarettes to offer each of the four a smoke. They respectfully declined.

'Do you come here every day?' he asked.

They nodded. One of them said: 'Unless there's a concert at Sarojini Naidu, the women's hostel. Then we go there.' You could tell from his sparkling sibilants and clear Hindustani, the sullenness and lazy tone, that he came from Allahabad town.

78

'And what happens when you get here?' quizzed Ashwin innocently, with no intent to patronize.

'We have tea, then samosas, and we look at the girls waiting to catch a train,' said the nice Bhojpuri lad from Udai's class, with a plainness to match.

'And then we drink more tea, and eat more samosas,' added the boy from Allahabad, on a note of defiance.

'I wonder what makes you come back here every evening,' said Ashwin. 'This town has many nice places. You must like watching trains?'

'There's that,' replied a third student, 'but this place is also close to the hostel. Tell us what *you* like about Prayag?' he urged Ashwin, perhaps to clarify his own thoughts.

'Oh, I like the noise of the place, its bustle. Coolies in red. A. H. Wheelers, and lots of people going somewhere. What are all of you planning to do ... after college, I mean?' Ashwin asked the Bhojpuri student. Mercifully, in this country you could still ask personal questions on a first acquaintance, or so he thought.

'Sit for the IAS exam,' replied the youth, automatically, without a pause.

'All of you?'

'All of us,' replied the boy firmly, with incredulity at Ashwin's question. Surely the lecturer knew how many men Allahabad fielded for the civil service each year?

The Allahabad man could stand it no longer. 'And what will you do, sir, with what you know about us? Put it all in a book?'

'Not yet,' grinned Ashwin. In his own slow-burning way, the young man was sharp. 'You haven't give me enough masala, have you? I hardly know the things that each of you thinks about.'

'Why should you?' said the youth, raising his eyebrows with a deliberate, light insolence. He had the measure of these young, liberal types. They wanted you to believe that you had freedom of expression, but were stung if you actually used it. 'The question is why should you? D'you think we're caged animals that you can sit and watch from the outside, and make notes about our feeding habits? The Indian who came back an Indophile, ever heard of that, boys?'

A boy muttered to him to shut up. The Bhojpuri apologized: 'Ignore what he says. The fellow's had a touch of the sun.' Ashwin watched the Allahabadi with a cool, pleasant interest.

'Don't stop him speaking, will you?' he pleaded. 'I want to hear what he has to say. He has a certain ... perspective on things.'

'Well, I shan't talk because you want me to. I refuse to be one of your case studies. What d'you want from us, anyway?'

'Let me see,' said Ashwin slowly. 'Since I'm new here, I suppose I want to make friends and find out about the things you enjoy doing. But since you mention it – as you talked – I *was* trying to figure out how life in this town could be made more interesting. There have to be more fun things here than tea, samosas and dull women heading out of town.'

'You've read a lot,' returned the youth. 'You've been to England, maybe even to other places, but do you understand anything about your own country? We hear that you talk to your students about class struggle and grabbing your opportunities, and not submitting to every social demand, but in a country this size, with just small pockets of industrial labour, can one ever really have a revolution? I doubt it. Where so many people live below the poverty line, can a man who offers its youth hope be in his senses? Hope, sir, is what my father had when he fought for India's freedom, but gagged on before I could even grow up.'

Ashwin had listened to him, attentive and motionless, thinking about China and the Soviet Union, when Udai suddenly roused himself and tugged at his sleeve: 'I think we should be going now, I'm expecting visitors. Where can this talk get us, anyway?'

Ashwin said that he wanted to walk home, he needed to think. Gandhi had done it, that frail bag of bones, the impossible work of ousting a conqueror race that lived here for two centuries, but which completely failed to identify with the dreams of its subject peoples. He had done it without bloodshed, but with an implacability before which all argument, even violence, failed. It was possible, thought Ashwin, to fight any enemy, unemployment, bad health, over-population – so long as enough people like himself decided to live together with the working classes, teaching them, working with their tools ... Gandhi was really a South African, who came to India in his late youth. It probably took an outsider to see most clearly the possibilities of action in this struggling, fatalistic country. In the West, whatever its ills, people never failed to try to pull themselves out of their misery. At least, by and by. Nothing was for ever, not family, not social expectation, not class, not even oneself ... Here, on the other hand, 'wisdom' consisted in recognizing that you were born to suffer, and in taking the suffering like a man. Also, passing on the stoicism rigorously to your son – as the necessary duty of a father. In this land of tribulations, ambition was the devil that lured with sweet words and stole your sanity, so it could break your will one day together with the gains of all past generations.

Softly, under his breath, Ashwin cursed fathers, Udai, himself, and then no one in particular. His ears rang still with the words of the student at Prayag. Can a man who offers our youth hope be in his senses? He turned into the lane leading up to the Misra home and was greeted with darkness, and people standing out on their doorsteps. There had been a power failure.

CHAPTER NINE

With my mind now set into a very definite cast (which, surely, in some part, L. Durrell and Cocteau had to answer for), it was time for certain old demons to come crowding in, flashing a buckle, making dawn, making day, wearing the mantle of experience this time ... I had come out of college with next to no skills and little appreciation of the everyday activity it took to hold a life together. Biren, who suspected my long hours of sleep, the reading and letter-writing, decided that I should get a taste of reality. He would send me to live in a modest home for some years, where I'd have family chatter and plenty of chores to pin my feet to the ground. And learn in the process how to make a good wife for someone.

A few years before this, Biren had left his job with the government, and set up in private practice at Banaras. He was a surgeon of repute by this time in the region of eastern UP, Bihar and Nepal, his fingers believed by the sick to possess properties of magic. He had quickly earned enough as a result to build a home and a small hospital for himself. The house still smelt of varnish and distemper, and was daily rocked by the drama of birth, death and recovery in the clinic two hundred yards away. All of us at home were nervous, prickly, keeping our own rooms and counsel despite the continual, despairing efforts of Ratna to bring us together. The solitariness had something to do with the unruly hours a doctor's home keeps, for there was seldom an evening or a meal at which all four of us were present in one place. Ratna ran the house and clinic with the aid of a small army of temperamental, slow-witted, opium- or spirit-ridden servants, as Sujit and I grew all the while more idle and grossly self-absorbed. And squeamish about dipping our fingers into life lest we turn either wicked or ugly. Which is when Biren despatched me to the home of his uncle, Sachi-mama, in Allahabad for post-graduate studies in English. Sachi-mama lived at 18 Church Lane with his wife Mami, some grandchildren and two daughters, Bela, friend of my childhood, and Sreela, her older sister. I went eagerly, expecting to form part of a noisy, cheerful home, where Bengali films and novels would be discussed over meals.

Mami's house cast a spell over me from the day I entered it. All its members, even the little children, were assigned proper duties, and appointed times when they would have to get up and do them. Each of us soon felt that, without our intervention, the household would come to a grinding halt. The girls, Bela and Sreela, sang ceaselessly, if without melody, as they worked, and even on the grimmest days (when Mami had ticked somebody off) there were loud arguments, music on the radio, and in the evenings a string of callers and wheezing laughter from Bela. After the silence and separatenesses of my father's home, I was struck by how much the sisters had to say in a day to each other, to me, even to outsiders. Nothing was too trivial or too private to be spoken. And all events, radio and newspaper announcements, visitors and weather alike, conspired volubly in the running of the

84

sparkling household, whose meaning lay woven somehow into the routine. Whose meaning perhaps was the routine.

In the night, the three-and-a-half-room house was metamorphosed into a giant dormitory, with mosquito curtains everywhere you looked. Mornings began at six when Bela and I sprang up to unhook, gather up and fold the night-time sets, leaving only a dull blue counterpane on a corner-room four-poster to conceal the soft, heaped contours of the household's last sleep. In the front room, there now appeared divans and a crop of low stools with printed cushions that were briskly dusted with a small broom. The cupboards stood crammed with books and a few featureless bibelots in marble or bamboo from Bankura or Krishnanagar. (It was in the living room with its dark red floor and cream-and-pink curtains fluttering prettily in the breeze that Bela and I spent most of our free time.) After a quick wash and change, we entered a dark prayer room (that doubled at other times as a dressing room or store) where Mami sat praying before a lighted picture of Radha-Krishna on a shelf. We prostrated with feeling to the God, then sat behind Mami and read shlokas out of the Bhagavad Gita. Soon it would be time for tea, and a cluster of us, women and children, would sit on white asanas in the kitchen, crunching Marie biscuits and listening to Vividh Bharati in the background. Commercials crackling through the interstices of romantic songs from the 'fifties, a radio clock and other ting-a-ling-a-lings. By ten, each of us had eaten a large meal and left for school, college or the local market, while Mami rushed off for lectures on the Gita to Colonelgunj, the neighbourhood where she was born.

The one who stayed behind was Sachi-mama, toothless sentinel, dozing over a newspaper with his glasses on, a silk shawl thrown lightly about his shoulders. He dreamed of the evenings when he had played bridge with Vijay-lakshmi Pandit, the tales he had told to Sarojini Naidu . . . Occasionally, Mami sent a child with money to him, and he would amble off in the same dreaming manner to buy mutton or oranges, to scold the milkman standing beside his buffalo for adding too much water to the milk. Mostly, he just sat till it was evening, when he would click his hard, smiling teeth into place and visit a certain Mrs Mitra in neighbouring Tagore town. Sachi-mama was sixty-five years of age, a retired railwayman on an exiguous pension, who had rubbed shoulders with famous women in his time – through his talent for bridge, a fund of gossip, and the unexpected good looks of a film star. His wife, who despised men who spoke out of turn and foraged continually for an audience of vain women, was not on speaking terms with him.

At the university, since most teachers were drawn from local talent and lacked a shred of inspiration, three classes out of four were frighteningly dull, part of a plan to numb our senses and arm them with fog for futures of tribulation. I sketched, wrote letters, even tried to lure my neighbours into written conversation, but they were listless, the men and women of my class, and stared with glazed eyes at the professor picking a corn off his knuckle or wiping the white corners of a despairing mouth. Alternatively, the keen ones made furious notes, bestowing an undeserved dignity upon some bad teacher's lonely drivel that never managed to connect the text with life at all. Which was tragic, for included in the course that year were *The Canterbury Tales*, *Doctor Faustus*, *King Lear*, *The Tempest*, *Sons and Lovers* and *Huckleberry Finn*.

In the evening, Bela and I plaited our hair, rubbed Basant Malati into our faces, and took a slow walk round the neighbourhood. Bela told stories out of Bengali films and Saratchandra, in which the men were always distant, awkward and moral, the women messes of self-destructive emotion. We walked till our calves hurt. At dusk, Mami blew the conch and we ran indoors to touch our foreheads to the cool floor before the illuminated god. Yet, despite the small beauties, the animation of Bela's lighted universe, when alone with my books or the spirits of the inner brain at night, secretly I began to fret. At the smallness of our concerns, and that nobody about me had any questions about why we engaged in this or that (or so much) activity. It was like living inside a bottle, safe, sanitized, but without the participation of the brain. I missed my friends from Lucknow, their unworldliness and rangy curiosity, their power to stimulate. I felt afraid that I would flap my wings in just such a cage for the rest of my life, and never break free of commonplaces. There was Vithal Sahai, head of English, of course, whom I was a little in love with ... The curling grey hair and perfectly timed drags on the pipe, his dry humour. He taught literary criticism, and is long dead now from a life of denying himself everything except books. He loved a woman writer, it was said, but she married and left for a cold country thousands of miles away. And wrote not a word afterwards. Poetry, said Vithal Sahai, does not save souls. It makes them, on the other hand, altogether worth saving.

Around three o'clock one December night, with the temperature around four degrees and frost on the window panes, I was dreaming about my Lucknow friend, Priti Singh, who had given me an expensive negligee for my birthday. Take a look at your sensual nose, she had said, the arrogant curve of your jaw. She had been sitting on a parapet in the January sun, reading a little jerkily from Andrew Marvell, when Bela shook me awake inside my thick cotton quilt.

'Wake up,' said Bela, eager to enlist my reserves for a family crisis. 'It's Dada. He's driven all the way up from Lucknow. His little daughters are with him, also a batman.'

Her brother, Nilratan Haldar. At this hour, I thought, unable without violence to unglue the sleep from my eyes. Or the astonishment, for ever since he had married that rich young woman, Monica somebody, he seemed to have forgotten his folks utterly. No letters to remind or reassure, no message from any quarter . . . yet here it was, an arrival in the dead of the night, intriguing like the rest of his life and pointedly dramatic.

He emerged from behind a screen (stirring slowly the giant flagstone of the past) in a camel-coloured mackintosh, the belt dangling by his side. The right foot was in a bandage, and on each arm he held a baby girl, blinking sleepily at the strange, whispering, owl-eyed shapes about them.

'Why are you here at this hour?' said a high-pitched Mami without conviction, wearing a little wearily the heroism thrust upon her by her earlier intransigencies. She had never yet seen, nor wished to see, the woman her son had married.

'I've left their mother,' he replied, in a voice lapped lightly by hysteria. 'She loathes me, my wife. And when she can't get to me sufficiently, she turns upon the children. Some things, she knows, will really hurt. Look at her arm . . . her mother burned her with a cigarette.' On the older child's lean limb were three brown rings, faint, close set; in her eyes the trustful smile of one who has long forgotten.

A gasp formed, ricochetting its way round the room

through Bela, Sreela, me ... cigarettes, brutality with children. Nilukaka looked into our faces with the expec-tation of one who has driven all night in the fog, and is rewarded at least by an answering shock in his listeners. Shock and outrage. Of course, the children would stay here, there was no question, his sisters seemed to say, we'll look after them. Sreela passed round steaming mugs of tea. In the centre of this human knot sat Sachi-mama with silk shawl and closed eyes, minus his teeth, saying nothing ... It was always up to Mami to decide what everybody would eventually think.

The batman entered with milk bottles, the babies' potties and slightly damp woollens, as Bela and Sreela took the infants from their brother's arms with clucks and practised pats. Mami, meanwhile, had slipped out of our midst and entered the prayer room for morning obeisances. It was the only way she could find to still her thudding heart and clear the morning brain for answers to an impossible occurrence.

'Take a good look at the little one,' she said to Bela and Sreela, a little too loudly from her dark retreat. The younger girl had deep blue eyes and watchfully sucked her tiny thumb. 'She isn't a year old yet,' continued Mami. 'An infant that age could die without her mother. I can't possibly take on the responsibility ... much too young the children are still. One has to think each step out clearly before one takes it.' Her voice had grown shriller with each phrase, gathering fast the fibres of panic.

Here was a decision. Things happened swiftly after that. It was barely an hour since they had arrived, already the orderly was taking the babies and bottles full of fresh milk back to a small car in the fog. Nilukaka stood under a naked bulb, his fine nose pink and watering slightly from the cold. He looked as always deep into my eyes and, through all his troubles, I glimpsed a corner that had taken note of, and was pleased to see, me. As if I was the world that had looked in on his personal miseries, and neither judged nor turned its back. I took, it seemed, the edge off his abasement. I touched his feet, squeezing his elbow afterwards to say, don't take it so hard, it'll turn out right in the end. He touched my cheek with his cold, troubled one. He smelt of powdered milk and, very faintly, whisky.

In the dark still, as suddenly as he had bodied forth (before, that is, his arrival could lay a proper claim upon our lives) he was gone. All of us excepting Mami returned to our snowy quilts. For a while, we heard no more from Nilukaka, only Mami listened now with lowered eyes and the deepest attention every time somebody mentioned her son ... As we rubbed cold cream into our faces at night, Bela and I spoke often of the wife Nilu had acquired against his mother's wishes, the unfathomable distance he kept from his parents. We said much at those times that did us no credit. Yet he had driven back quite readily to Lucknow, where a whole life, whatever its pitfalls, awaited him. Perhaps his wife had waited up all that night, sleepless and full of remorse ... What we suspected was attention-getting and demands from her of an order that no husband could fulfil, that she wanted – not just his presence – but his whole soul. Yet, clearly, there were gaps in the story we conjured that our experience could not yet fill.

CHAPTER TEN

Ashwin sat hunched one night over a lesson he was reading for the next class. The Wars of the Roses. He didn't know that he wouldn't be talking history to his pupils tomorrow, but about the Labour Party in England, the trade union movement in that country. There was disaffection in the working classes still, but listing now towards higher material prospects ... the twenty-one-inch colour telly, a house in Hertfordshire; perhaps some gaudy furniture on the hire purchase that wouldn't be do-it-yourself any more. They were getting dreadfully bourgeois, British workers, not that he would mention such a thing in class. He thought of Susan. Now Susan couldn't be bourgeois in a fingernail, and not all the education in the world make her so. He thought of last summer at Howgill Fells, just outside the Lake District. Susan and he had rented a caravan about three miles from a village, and spent a week of long walks and lazing with bread, ham, cheese and wine, and a feast of Mendelssohn on their little portable. A farmer with a beautiful white beard had passed each morning with his pail of milk, but seemed not to notice Susan at all, sitting in the doorway without a stitch on her. She had a high colour, and her hair smelt of honey, spilling as it did in waves upon the plump goblets of her breasts. One afternoon, as they walked to the top of a hill, there had been a terrible cutting wind, and Susan putting her hands into his pockets: 'Can we, here, with those goats watching?' she had whispered. He had found her warm in a very wet cleft, and had feared a little freezing his bottom, but she got on top, and it had been very nice. The goats were later joined by a young man in patched tweeds, watching with bucolic serenity an ungainly species of animal mating in the grass, but they were too close to the end to care.

It was getting on for ten. Ashwin heard the scrape of hard bony shoes in the courtyard as Beni Madho returned home, his soft burblings as he washed his feet and hands at the indoor pump. Afterwards, for the whole night, there would be silence. The remarkable thing about the Misra marriage, thought Ashwin, was its flat, unending silence. The woman either waiting for or on Beni Madho like a deaf-mute, leaning her head to one side. Suddenly, tonight, he heard murmurs, and Damyanti's voice, peevish, raised above the ordinary.

'What are you doing with my clothes? Leave them alone. You're ruining my things.'

'You tell me then,' said Beni Madho's turbid voice, revealing an insufficient grip over the vowels. 'I know you take money from the housekeeping . . . it has to be in the house. I'll find it if I have to tear the place apart.'

'What a calamity,' cried Damyanti. 'There isn't any money, I told you.'

'Liar. Where did you get the stuff when Urmila's daughter was married? Buying her earrings, as if I don't notice. Squandering my wages on two-paisa neighbours. And when Bapu had to be cremated, who came out with five hundred rupees? In front of the headmaster, too. Making me look like a miser. Give me the money.'

'I stopped saving when Bapu died,' replied Damyanti, with a prim mendacity. 'I've no use for it now. My mother even sends clothes twice a year.' In a small, clear voice that cracked like a whip across the night, she then asked: 'What do you want it for?'

'I've creditors to pay off,' said Beni Madho, whining with impatience, 'a mahajan.'

'Creditors, haan?' said Damyanti, slow and sarcastic. 'What mahajan wants his money at this hour? Maybe you can tell me his name.'

'Arre ja, what do you understand. I won't stand here answering questions all night. And *you* should ask . . . living off my earnings all these years, no gratitude even. Will you give what you have or . . .?'

There was a crash, followed by the bump and rich roll of round shapes, beads and bowls, as they scattered and came to rest at different rhythms upon an uneven floor. 'You've broken it,' screamed Damyanti, 'you've broken my mother's paandaan.' She used it as a cask for her little treasures, anklets, bead necklaces, a carved bowl. 'It's for that dancing girl you want my money, don't you? How long will you hold her wild glance with flattery and small gifts? There are young men with gold in this city. In tolas, fat bangles. Will she spit on your face once she meets one of them? I gave you all I had, my labour, my youth . . .' She clutched at her stomach as it squirted and burned, humiliation's black bile.

Beni Madho rose with a snarl. Young men, he thought, will never match my tenderness or experience, my Sanskrit. What a woman really wants is cherishing and little jokes, and poetry. He clattered out of the house again, clutching the gathers of his dhoti with one hand, with the other, a small silver bowl.

What made married people, mused Ashwin, more

brutal with each other than they were to any stranger? Yet they clung like limpets to the institution. Why, he wondered, did Beni Madho keep a wife? Next morning, as he ate a paratha in the kitchen, he asked Damyanti, hesitating:

'Have you ever thought of putting your money in the bank, mausi? You've some jewellery, too, I presume. Put it all in.' The hesitation came not from a feared indelicacy, but because he wished to avoid tears first thing in the morning.

'If I ask Misraji to put it into his account, I can bid farewell to the money that day.'

'I didn't mean that,' said Ashwin quickly. 'You could open an account in your name, Damyanti Misra. The money will earn an interest annually, and when you're old, you'll have yourself a little pension.'

Her eyes widened with mistrust, the suspicion of turpitude in her source of wisdom. 'You mean, I should make savings separately from Beni Madho ... I can't do that. He'd kill me if he found out.'

'Think about it,' said Ashwin, leaping up to wash his hands. He looks a shaitan, mused Damyanti, the devil as he must have looked when he was young. Putting me up to things against my own husband. 'Who can tell,' the lecturer went on, unmindful of making waves, 'if you have money of your own, Misraji might begin to listen to you a bit.'

In a trance, she stirred milk in the big aluminium pot, round and round and round. That was something men understood, money, they quivered to its power, coming to life before its heavy, toneless jingle. They didn't sneer at women who had a few thousand put away.

'I've never seen the inside of a bank,' said Damyanti

Misra, raising crafty eyes, but the devil had left for the university, and was late for his first class.

Around four one afternoon, she went up to Ashwin's room to put away some shirts she had ironed. He would be back from class any moment, she thought, making a mess in the kitchen. Brewing tea in the way he had, six minutes in the pot, with cold milk added later. Cold milk! Damyanti started. On the bed with his face in the pillow was the lodger, clad in last night's pyjamas. Damyanti coughed at the door.

He twisted his head, screwing up his eyes into sightless, black stones. Who was it? What was this woman doing, pottering about in his room? His head hurt, he wished that she would go away. Damyanti switched on the fan, and picked up a dirty teacup.

'You've been in all day,' she said in accusation, 'and come down for neither breakfast nor lunch. Are you sick? The heat is awful, Urmila's son . . .'

'I'm all right.' He cut her short. Why was she standing there still? All these months, the beauty of this woman had been her reticence, her lack of chatter.

'Nor did you eat dinner last night,' she observed, sticking firmly to food for proof of misconduct. 'You pay good money, shouldn't you at least eat your meals regularly?'

'Yes,' he mumbled, with closed eyes, his nose in the pillow. 'I'd like to be left alone, if you don't mind. I don't feel much like talking.'

Slowly, she descended the stairs, her limbs heavy in the hot sun. Damyanti felt again as she had done for many years, failed and nerveless. Had she said something wrong?

95

One thing was clear, the fellow always had a surprise for you. Suddenly, Ashwin called:

'I'll be down for dinner tonight. I'm not going out.'

Last evening, after months of wondering and a dry, rustling fear, there had been a letter from Susan:

Darling Ashwin,

This tardy note as I had first to get things straight in my own head. I shan't after all be able to leave it all — Surrey, my parents, roast beef and Yorkshire pud on Sundays, all the small things — and come away to a big, unknown land to live with you. It's not that I don't love you (I can't believe that I shall ever feel this sharp intensity with another), it's that I don't love you enough to give up the details of a life that I know and understand so well. The ways of people in our two countries are so bewilderingly dissimilar.

Give my love to your father, the dear man. When I wrote each year to 'pay him my respects', I was always invaded by a sense of unreality . . . I could never be as good as he wanted me to be. I would want my Ashwin scuffling and rolling on top of me on the living-room carpet right in the middle of some foetid family quarrel. That's silly, but I think you'll understand — since you couldn't live away from India either. There's nobody else yet, but Mother thinks it better in the circumstances that we don't keep in touch. I agree.

Much love.

By the end, Ashwin had first felt drained, and then as if a tight, brown sack that he'd held off unconsciously for weeks was now being drawn swiftly over his head. No time even for a last wish. He lay awake in one posture the whole moonless night, all dream snuffed out of him.

At two o'clock one night in Oxford, when Ashwin was typing out his thesis, Susan had come yawning out of bed with an offer of coffee, wearing one of his shirts. Her nipples were big and rosy from sleep ... He would never put his face between those big brown thighs again, he thought, and where the brown gave place to the tenderest, startling white. They had made love in the shower and in the kitchen in the early days, even on a night bus to Surrey ... Susan would laugh at Ashwin's plan to teach Indians about political power, the new teaching methods he upheld, involving continuous dialogue with the pupil. He ached (as he read Paulo Freire) to hear the thoughts that Indians had about themselves now. They had to be different from what their fathers or political leaders told them. Egghead, she called him, mussing his hair, you should have been a Tamil called Ramaswamy, and stormed the stuffy mathematics department with shy, earth-shaking formulae. We'd have laughed at you, and left you alone. I shan't have my children corrupted by your seriousness, their fun taken out of life. He had wondered at the time how much of it she meant, but stopped short of asking her. She might think he had no humour left in him at all.

What would Susan make of his life with the Misras, he wondered now. Needlessly bolshie, she would say, you don't have to rough it all the time to be a serious person. She didn't understand. The only way to grasp the concerns of a class, their special worries, was by living their life. He could talk to his students with authority now, from the vantage point of rock-hard reality ... It occurred to him that, as things stood, Susan wouldn't get to see Damyanti at all. Or Beni Madho of the stained teeth and heavy, swaying walk, the love songs he sang nightly under his breath:

My bracelet, it keeps slipping off,
My lover hath cast a spell upon me...

Ashwin suddenly felt a jabbing hunger, the first unsentimental demand of his lean body for several hours. He would ask the lady downstairs for food. First, however, he needed a bath to rid his unslept limbs of their corrupting numbness, the sharp, sour smell of last night's pain.

As he came down, Damyanti was soaking a cement platform in the centre of the courtyard with jets of water from a limp hosepipe. Still later, he emerged from his wash and watched Damyanti myopically mend Beni Madho's mulmul kurtas, sitting on the ground. Three wet straw mats lay drying about her. Ashwin fetched himself some tea and biscuits, and lowered himself on to one of the cool chatais. In the dimming light, she held a garment close up to check whether the stitches were in a straight line. They sat in silence for a while.

'I told you a lie,' he said at last. 'I don't have a mother. She died in childbirth when I was three years old.'

'What does it matter,' said Damyanti, startled, 'whether you told the truth or a lie? I've got my own work to do.' Who was the cuckoo clock for then? And who brought Ashwin up as a boy?

They could no longer see each other's faces, turning into dark and comfortable shapes, just out of arm's reach for each other in the courtyard.

'I got a letter from Susan yesterday,' said Ashwin, too casually, hoping she would let it pass.

She didn't. 'The firangi? Is she coming to India?'

'No ... no. That's what the letter's about, in fact,' he replied evenly. 'Susan won't be coming any more, she's left me.'

She repeated his words slowly to herself, in an effort to grasp their meaning, then: 'Does she say she won't marry you ... after living under the same roof? Doesn't sound like a good girl to me.'

'Now, now, mausi,' said the young man, 'let's not take it too fast. It isn't a crime to turn a fellow down.'

'She was your wife ... more than. You said you talked to her about everything.'

He was silent at first. 'Wives, it is clear,' he said in a voice that dug an abyss of grief, 'leave their husbands after the time of happiness is over.'

'Do women really walk out?' said Damyanti, in tones of vapid amazement. 'Where will she go now, Soosan? What man will take her who deserted you?'

Ashwin gave a bark of laughter, throwing his head back to spy the North Star that was making a tentative, peeping foray into the glossy evening. 'You're unbelievably stupid,' he said. 'Susan will go out and fend for herself like any man you know. She'll marry some day.' Inwardly, this smarted. 'Not that this other guy will be half as clever or as interesting as I am, but till then she doesn't have to belong to anybody. It's rubbish, you know, this business of belonging ... his wife, their children. Does Misraji belong to you? We aren't ceiling fans or bicycles, it's each one on his own. Which is probably our strength.' My words, he thought dizzily, are out of a failed comedy tonight, they're a lie ... I'm alone, my thoughts are muddy, and from the way my legs feel, I don't think I can walk up the stairs again.

Damyanti peered into his face in the weak light, it looked chalky and drawn. As if nobody had ever loved him in all his twenty-seven years, she thought, a little mawkishly.

'It's not that Susan doesn't love me,' said Ashwin, ironing out before Damyanti the puckers of a resolute weakness, holding them down. 'If I asked you to go and live where they spoke a foreign tongue, or ate beef and bread and potatoes, would you go?' She shook her head. Not that anybody would ever ask. 'Nor would I,' he sighed. It came over him again, the unreality of a few moments ago, eating at his root, all he believed in. The pain of last night rose once again with its low, seamless moan. It seemed impossible at this moment that other things (knowledge, action, sex) would ever gain mastery over this sensation, his distended, throbbing self.

It was wholly dark by this time. Damyanti rose to light an earthen lamp by the tulsi sapling nearby, joining her palms before it. From the house next door came the sound of conches crying nasally three times, the call to mid-evening prayer.

'I've begun singing again,' announced Damyanti. 'It's nearly four weeks since I started riaz ... ever since Urmila's son had the taanpura strung. I wait till you and Misraji leave in the morning, I don't bathe or wash up in the kitchen, just start singing right away ... The ragas are coming back, it's my voice that's slow in catching up.' When Ashwin didn't reply, she said: 'Don't move, I'll go and fetch my taanpura.'

She sat afterwards, a hand opening and closing to a slow beat, the other on the strings, taking the first meditative notes of the bhairavi. It was an old Manna Dey song, plangent, sentimental:

> *'Ask me not how I passed the night,*
> *Each moment drawn out to an age,*
> *At the end of which, sleep was nowhere in sight.'*

Ashwin lay down on a wet mat (which wasn't long enough, so he had to bend his knees). The woman's grave voice reverberated in the thick, soft night with the power of a rich violin. A small breeze had begun to rustle its infant feathers.

> *'My breast burns here, and there a lamp,*
> *Dispelling not the darkness of my home ...'*

From a corner of Ashwin's face rolled some slow, fat tears into the mat's sated straw. About him was the absorbent darkness, and Damyanti poised upon a needle, singing with closed eyes. It was a bhajan in pilu now, then a couplet in bhairavi, and all the while the breeze cooling, lifting, bringing to rest.

Beni Madho came in earlier than usual, around eight thirty. Damyanti was busy in the kitchen, and did not emerge to follow him to the bedroom in the way she had, with her sad, accusing eyes. In the courtyard lay the incredible lodger, curled up on a mat too small for him, the slow-warming ground. A giant taanpura squatted before him on its shining gourds, astir and full of secrets in the dark. Fellow's come from England to learn our lowly arts, said Beni Madho to himself. They gave you pleasure, these trifles, one had to admit. His mind turned naturally to Chandibai, Ujala's mother, who sang sometimes with glorious dancing eyes to accompany her daughter's spirited kathak.

'Wake up, sir,' said Beni Madho, 'the night is young. You can't sleep your life away.'

CHAPTER ELEVEN

In March, with the quilts stored away but not yet our silk saris, when we hesitated still to renounce hot baths for cold showers, I awoke in the front room one mild morning and found a man sitting at the table by the window. It was Major Haldar, and I had overslept. In another room, Bela and the others were already at prayer to Mami's chanting and the intermittent tinkle of a small bell. I wore what we called a duster coat in those days, a buttoned-up overall in a sap-green-and-white cotton, reaching down to the knees. He was smoking a cigarette and watched me body forth from behind the mosquito curtain, legs, duster coat, face and tousled hair, in that order.

'Hello,' I said, still half-asleep, walking up to touch his feet. 'Have you been here long?' He shook his head.

As I straightened up, he placed an arm about my hip and drew me close, leaning his cheek lightly upon my breast. I breathed still the deep, even breaths of sleep, and through the cloth, his skin was cool against the warm, slow-waking loaf of my body. Eventually, it pierced my morning stupefaction that something with a hot, sharp breath was about, a slinky, unexpected red beast stirring and stirring in its lair ... My body had lost its old boniness, and a grown man's head now nestled on one of its more intimate curves. Getting through not just to my body but to something more disturbing, my feelings, which went back to puberty, when such things still shocked but drove in with the power of a newly primed sword. I drew away.

He threw his head back to look up at my face, but the forearm stayed firm about my hip. It was confusing and it was nice. I moved further away still, making the enquiries that would restore to the association its old daylight civility. Keeping the loveliness of the man intact without the intrusion of a disturbing particularity, his touch. How were the children, I asked. His wife? Where was he posted now?

'Lucknow,' he replied to the last. I thought of two little girls with dark, burning eyes and narrow faces, the cruelty of a December fog. 'We shan't be there much longer, though. I'm expecting a posting quite soon.'

'Where to?' it seemed natural to ask. 'Will you be going to Delhi?'

'No,' he murmured, looking out of the window, 'I don't really know yet.' You could tell from the way his face closed, his stubbing out a cigarette roughly, with finality, that he knew exactly where. Not that his reply mattered to me particularly, just the mystery, and his need to conceal. 'How are Biren-da and Boudi, your wonderful parents?' he quickly asked, steering the conversation to regions of safety, where sudden questions had no power to block the sun.

'Very well,' I replied. 'Baba, you might have heard, resigned from the government some years ago, and set up on his own in Benares, a truly dull old town. Ma and I gripe all the time, but his reputation as a surgeon came in handy there when he started a private practice. He's also built a house and hospital now that you must go and see.'

'I intend to ... quite soon. Biren-da must be rich now. I'm really happy that he quit his job. The government is a place strictly for the mediocre, where people around feel threatened by signs of talent. And if they stumble upon some undeniable evidence that a man is first rate, they usually punish him for it.'

'Baba certainly inspired great hostility in his seniors,' I answered. 'He isn't too tactful himself, but you should have seen what they did to him, his bosses, flinging him out to all sorts of remote places where he would have no work at all. He just wanted to teach surgery in a medical college, and be where he was needed, with the sick. Wealth hasn't done much for his temper, mind you, it's worse than ever. He works twelve hours a day ... but tell me about yourself. What are you doing? I hadn't heard of a cavalry regiment in Lucknow.'

'There isn't one,' replied Nilukaka. 'Nobody seems to know this, but I left the armoured corps years ago. Promotions in that wing are so slow that you never get beyond the rank of colonel. Right now, I'm handling operations for the eastern sector, overall planning, that sort of thing.'

'And what brings you to Allahabad?' I enquired, hoping that he was home on holiday.

He stiffened, a porcupine of caution once again, as if I had asked after his bank balance. 'Nothing special,' he presently said. 'A small piece of official work.' At nine o'clock, an army jeep arrived to fetch Major Haldar, and two armed guards sat themselves on either side of him. I was dressing for morning class and didn't know that, three kilometres from the house, Nilukaka would switch over to another military vehicle. An olive green ambassador with shaded windows, a new set of escorts, and a man on a motorbike piloting their gravid progress. Later I was to understand that on that morning, Nilukaka had carried with him plans and papers of the highest importance, which would go one day to create a new nation. That morning, with my natural numbness to fact and outward events, that's all it was still, a small piece of official work.

At three, when I returned from college, Nilukaka was innocently asleep on a divan in the front room. I stood beside him as he awoke, describing the afternoon lecture on Dryden, which the professor's genius had transformed into a subject as interesting as drainage systems for Indian cities in the nineteenth century. The boys in the back row had openly slept. I told Nilukaka about Tara and Kavita, two very pretty girls, who made copious notes in class and would bring the same assiduity and wide eyes to their homes and marriages one day. Nilu said:

'You're so grown up now, I get a little shock each time I look at you.' I saw him loose upon my arms, shoulders, throat and breasts a keen and unabashed attention.

'Don't,' I snapped. 'Please, don't.' I have never accepted with grace (from either man or woman) a close appraisal of my person. It isn't fear most times, just the swift recoil from being viewed as a thing, a cow at a cattle fair. At nineteen, I was still relatively unaware of my body, its frailties and power, and I wasn't going to let anybody change that. It was others I wanted to see leaping and arching their backs, blowing kisses and laughing, with reddening faces. I believe that it is from the day we become fully conscious of the flesh, and think about its aches, its terrible beauties and needs, that the process of ageing begins . . . Nilukaka changed the subject.

In a while, I brought up what was on my mind. I owed the family something. 'You're home after five years,' I said. 'Mami's in there, reading her prayer book. She's even missed a prayer meeting, something I've never seen her do. Won't you go in and talk to her? About anything, just like you're talking to me.'

He looked disturbed. 'I'd do that,' he murmured, two faint lines appearing beside his mouth, 'if I'd ever had a chat with Ma in my life. I can't somehow see myself beginning at the age of thirty-two.'

'You've no idea how the woman dotes on you. I've watched her closely, she goes quiet (with an unbearable kind of happiness) the moment Bela and I begin to talk about you. Mami doesn't speak, she just wants us to go on and on, and never get on to another subject. She really wants you to make up with her, you know. Couldn't you bring Monica and the children down some time?'

He lay on his back, taking slow drags on a cigarette, staring at the ceiling. His jaws were heavy, I saw crow's-feet around the eyes and, above the belt, the gentle beginnings of a pitiless paunch. It seemed sad that a giant of my childhood now had a trivial vice, he smoked. It indicated other stresses, other flaccidities of the spirit, of which I could have no knowledge.

'I wasn't yet fifteen,' he said, 'when I finished school. Ma pushed me into Khadakvasla at that age, and made a soldier out of me. I might have had other plans, abilities, a different future, but my mother ground them to a fine dust that day.'

I nodded. 'Somehow I can't help feeling that Mami did the best she could. She wasn't too well educated herself, and with Sachi-mama's hopeless indifference, it was the only way she could guarantee a stable life for you. Were you good at studies in school?'

'No,' he replied, 'not at all. But then I was horsing around with a hockey stick most of the time. Or with rich boys who had unmentionable things on their minds.'

'Nobody seems to get what they want. Take my parents,' I said. 'They hardly talked to me when I was a child. They tended me in different ways, but I was fed, kept warm, instructed, and then tucked gently away. So I took to speaking with other adults, mainly when my parents weren't listening. For to Biren and Ratna, children who spoke in front of adults were insufferable pests. Sometimes, I would hear my father say to Ratna: "Megha really knows how to impress people. The Kauls are raving about her." My behaviour would suddenly be cheapened by those words, made corrupt. As if I was having people on. Each time, I thought, why is it you can't see anything in me? You, too, might like it if you just stopped to listen. Then I entered my teens, and overnight my mother wanted me to start talking to her about my preoccupations, be her friend. I would have laughed if I wasn't somehow smashed up inside. Ma would actually cry before her sisters about having such an unnatural daughter, one who neither offered confidences nor revealed her feelings in any matter. It was strange that she couldn't see how I was by then, with a whole completed universe inside. I could manage without her or anybody ... that's what I thought at the time. Something must have made me that way.'

'So we march into adult life,' smiled Nilukaka, a painted clown in a bad play, knitting untidy eyebrows, 'still looking for the mother we needed when we were really babies.'

Yours loves you deeply, sadly, I'll testify to that, I

thought. I was the one who wanted a mother to care about me madly, uncontrollably, no matter how wicked or ugly I was. Who – when I came home – would neither ask questions nor go through my papers for clues to who I was, just sit quietly, rubbing oil into my hurting scalp. My failure, as I saw it, was in not being able to inspire love like that in anybody. So now I wanted to do things, marvellous things, and prove to somebody that I was worthy of attention. Which was absurd, I knew. For personal worth begets not love, it begets admiration.

'What I wanted,' said Nilu quietly, reliving some scene from the past, 'was a mother to love me beyond her little ego. Mine kept away because of her pride, she never could come off her high moral pedestal.'

I sat on the floor, hugging my knees, excited at having discovered a person who searched for the same thing as I, a prodigal love. 'Mind you,' I added, withdrawing into sanity, the premises by which one would survive, 'I wouldn't change my folks for anybody else's. As an adolescent, I used to think mine overbearing, insensitive and full of themselves, then I saw the parents my friends had. Soon, my own began to stand out as gentle, good people who admired learning and excellence. Who even had a feeling for beauty.'

'Your parents are marvellous,' said Nilukaka, clucking with impatience. 'You should see the people I'm sur-rounded by nowadays, my wife's relatives. They're rich, they're westernized, and about as cultivated as spuds waiting under the earth.'

The air filled with the smell of chameli and burning joss sticks as Mami entered the prayer room. 'What's your wife really like?' I asked. It just slipped out, the indis-cretion, intended to glean from him merely the truth of his whole existence.

'Oh, she,' he said, shutting his eyes in the way his father had, obliterating with one gesture the difficulty before him. 'Well, she's really warm and impulsive one minute, and completely destructive in the next. Like a wild animal ... sometimes I think she'll swallow me. We'll not talk about her.' The eyes remained closed a long time. Nilukaka went back to Lucknow the same night.

CHAPTER TWELVE

Soon it was 1971, and my first year MA examinations were late. I should have gone home to Benares in April, but with the demon sun devouring the yellow grass and naked poor outside, indoors, the prickly heat and tempers gone mad, I sat writing examinations in June. As in earlier years, I had paid scant attention to the course, so I paced up and down before each paper now, muttering in a dark-ringed dementia, reading out of the notes of the shiny-haired Tara and Kavita the numerous obfuscations of literary theory. It was trying, and all I thought of, indeed craved passionately at that point, was sleep, a deep, insensible, week-long quietus.

In the midst of the ink stains and fuss, my fitful sleep and swinish eating (examinations, I find, increase the appetite disgustingly), arrived Major Haldar, doubtless on some secret mission again. I cannot say what he did with himself for the first few days. I either moped with a book in some corner over my lakes of ignorance or sat in a state of shock in the university halls before some examiner's barbaric curiosity, his penchant for useless fact. In the evening, when the temperatures dropped, I came up to the terrace and with a table lamp for witness, read without hope into the night. Occasionally, I would chance upon a connection, that between Man and relentless Nature, the 'trick' by which a favourite story worked, even the peculiar way in which a character expressed a motive. I would get restless to speak with somebody at such times, but in that city there really was no one. (I discovered only years later that I had – quite unnecessarily – a down on Allahabad. For no matter what city you are in, in the instant of being seized by an idea, there never is anybody to tell it to. And if there was, those of us trained to silence would still not speak from fear of either incomprehension in the listener or worse, being seen to be – in some way – sentimentalizing the obvious.)

Sometimes, as I read after dinner, Nilukaka would pull a camp bed up to my lamp, lighting a cigarette, and read a paperback. It was usually something forgettable, an ash blonde with tawny eyes purring on a cover of dappled maroon. He never started a conversation, just handed me cold water if he brought a bottle up, or picked up the pencils and paper that flew out of my nerveless grasp. If we spoke, it was when I wanted a break. We laughed at cousins or dreamed aloud in the steamy night about the cool, curling mountains of Garhwal. Once he said something about marriage ... 'It really isn't all it's cracked up to be. Today, I'm sure of only one thing, it doesn't pay to deny one's roots.' Except I had examinations to think of, a crowded brain, and couldn't stop to abet somebody's growing disaffection.

The night before the fiction paper, I stood peering in clouded lamplight at Smollett, Swift and Dickens with distaste and fear. There was a Freudian analysis of *Sons and Lovers*, and somebody dredging up the ultimate sociological truth from *David Copperfield*. In the midst of which (cant and heavy weather), Nilukaka asked a question, something companionable, are you hungry, can I bring up a snack? With my tinder pent and tightly packed that moment, I went off: Don't speak to me. Can't you see I'm going crazy? I know nothing, absolutely nothing, for tomorrow's paper. He placed a forefinger on his lips, and mimed a hurtling, tiptoe exit from the terrace. Every so often after that, I would see his eyes leave the book he held, and turn upon my face. I stood up sometimes, sighing, pulling my hair, reading an indigestible gobbet aloud, and, each time, he would reach out from where he lay to hold (lightly, with two fingers) the hem of my skirt. (When I went downstairs, he would sleep on a camp bed on the terrace.) As I put my books away, I asked him to wake me up next morning at four. Do you promise? If you don't remember, I shall surely fail . . . He looked that night as if he would promise me anything at all in the world.

Around four, he shook me lightly by the feet. I rose and tore an angry sleep out of my eyes with cold water. Once again, in what was still feeble light, I began pacing up the terrace, a ghost with unsettled scores, worrying a closely scribbled exercise book in my hands . . . If Thomas Hardy's mind had a gloomy cast, and none of his characters could get things right, he could at any rate have avoided writing so many books. There was worse, the exuberant Henry Fielding, and the tendency of the unforgiving Swift to satirize his fellow men. Nilukaka brought up a cup of tea. Is it better, he asked. A quarter of the course still unread, I shook my head. With examinations, it was never going to be better. Nor was I able to cope with sociability at that moment. He looked sadly into my eyes, searching for something, the old attention, a promise of future warmth? I could hardly share with him (then or later) the gritty, untameable stuff of my concerns, so I just looked desperate. He touched my shoulder and went back to bed.

The paper went off well. There were, when all was said, George Eliot and Lawrence, Jane Austen and Virginia Woolf, holding up their end of the parti-coloured canopy with thrilling billows and eddies of image or meaning. I left out the jargon and sat back, thinking about life and the ways by which it was revealed, the authors' compulsions, and when it came to characters, what was psychologically true ... The connections fell into place, and by the third question, something like pleasure grew to accompany an aching hand. I went home quickly, and was sucked into a deep, drowning sleep in the front room with its dark red floor.

It was three thirty when I awoke. The windows had been darkened against a malevolent, whewing heat and wind that stalked the verandah, while indoors the ceiling fans whispered the traditional cooling fables of summer to our sleep. Bela, her sister and the children lay around me, sleeping like the dead. Mami was away at a prayer meeting, and from the next room came the snores of Sachi-mama, keening like a soft, unloved fiddle. Where was Nilukaka? Why wasn't he asleep somewhere like the rest? An intolerable silence hung in the air. Something waited in June's prickling warmth, despite June's warmth, holding its culprit breath. I went looking for him.

He was reading his trashy paperback in a corner room, feet up on a facing cane chair, a table fan trained upon him. His khaddar kurta looked as if it hadn't been ironed for days. Nilukaka looked up as I entered, his eyes questing once again for something in mine.

'What are you doing?' I asked.

'Reading a philosophical treatise, as you can see,' he affably replied. 'I wish I could sleep as easily as some.'

'Right,' I said, arch, knowing perfectly the outcome. 'I'm just loafing. I'll let you get on with your reading.'

'No,' he was quick. 'You stay. I'm reading this garbage for want of better occupation.' We spoke in undertones to keep from waking the rest. He reached out for my hand in the old companionate way, but his own was hot, disturbing. I sat down on the floor beside him, wearing the old, pale green-and-white duster coat.

We chatted at first desultorily, about nothing in particular, then he said: 'Haven't you got a boyfriend?' I shook my head. 'The way you look now, I'm surprised you haven't half a dozen young men hanging about you. How about the boys in your class?'

'Oh, them.' I made a face. 'Most of them can't tell their right hand from their left. Sometimes, I feel old enough to be their mother.'

Nilukaka smiled. 'You are, let's see, nineteen years old, is that right? Surely there's been somebody in all these years that you've liked better than the rest. In that special way?'

'There was,' it came out slowly, 'someone I grew quite fond of in Lucknow ... it seems a long time ago.' I was lying. We saw no young men at the convent, and thought the ones we ran into at parties puerile and savage. I wasn't going to reveal my inexperience though, a repellent vice, before this smooth, expansive man of the world.

'Tell me who it was,' said Nilu at once, begging and all peculiar. 'Maybe I can speak to your parents about him?'

I shook my head and looked sadly into the cruel distance, the impossibility of happiness ... I was in fact afraid of what I would find to say if he decided to probe. If he forced out the details, one by one. He probed not at all, but bent down instead, and placing his hands swiftly beneath my elbows, lifted them on to his lap. Suddenly, I was in a huddle upon his thighs, our faces close. I was afraid to breathe. Lightly, he kissed a dull, burning cheek, and my hair tumbled out of its rubber band on to my hunched shoulders. When he kissed my cheek again, he left a casual wetness there, a mild question ... beside us throbbed a rickety black fan, its blades threatening to come off with each revolution. I waited, trying to figure out the source of my alarm, my sense-erasing confusion, then his mouth was on mine, that beautiful fleshy bow, kissing me deeply, making my face all moist. I closed my eyes. When (after a year) I opened them again, I found his half-closed ones watching me with a fugitive smile in their depths, perhaps a tenderness. Suddenly, our years of reticence were upon me, their incalculable, dry safety. I said 'dhut' and, wiping an all-wet mouth, fled the room. In the evening, he asked would I walk with him to a little shop down the road for a Coke. I refused. There was just so much sensation you could take at a time.

The British history paper was now two days away so I went back to the terrace that night with lamp and Trevelyan, pencils and a hopelessly slump-backed canvas chair, my face warm from lack of sleep. The air was still, the lamp giving off an unbearable heat, and neither companionable natter nor Nilukaka pulling his camp bed up to wherever I sat any more. It stood in the bleak centre of the large terrace, a mosquito curtain tucked tightly about it. Snuffing out for ever the gentle neither-nor quality of earlier evenings, bespeaking a fever between two people now. Nilukaka stood at the far end of the dark terrace, revealed only by his cigarette's orange tip. I read on for a while, but when my brain ceased to connect (first, consecutive sentences, then contiguous words), I switched off the lamp and walked across to him. We said nothing for a long time, then I:

'Before the exams, Bela and I walked here every night till our calves hurt, and we were ready to sleep. The heat gets her down now. Will you walk once round the terrace with me?'

'Of course,' he murmured. The roof with its maps in black and grey was bathed in a pale, unwavering moon light. By the third round, he was holding my hand. Slowly, we walked to the bed. Slower still, he pulled out a fold of the mosquito curtain and sat himself on the cot's edge.

'It's awkward to have you standing there,' said Nilu Haldar. 'Won't you come and sit with me?'

I hesitated, briefly, the maws of eventuality upon us. 'I . . . I don't know. I'm afraid.'

'Why is that? Were you afraid this afternoon?'

'I'm a virgin,' I blurted to a face in shadow, getting the worst over, and stood afterwards numb and revealed.

'You'll come to no harm,' he coaxed, pulling me gently by the arm. He lay then on his side as I sat with careful calculation against his patient stomach. He combed the hair away from my face with light, strong fingers.

After an age, he said: 'Surely you can see how I feel about you. I'm a little shaken seeing you so grown up, so lovely . . . it's taken me a few days to get used to the sensation: I think I love you,' he quietly announced, and kissed my wooden shoulder. When I said nothing, he sat

117

up and slowly, resolutely devoured my mouth and eyelids. 'What are you thinking?' he asked, suddenly nervous. Had he made a mistake?

'I was thinking,' I replied, 'that I've liked you in this way for years . . . since I first went to college.' I was lying again. I had adored this man culpably, thrilling to his touch, since I was a child. From the edges of the night, there started a gentle breeze, warm still but laced with the heady fragrance of chameli.

'I had no idea,' he exclaimed, not without his own share of untruth. 'Why haven't you told me before?'

I ducked, unable to explain that he had been too beautiful, too much in charge, for a twelve-year-old to tell her love to. Nor had I then the words. So I said: 'You were an uncle, remember, or shouldn't one remind you?'

Slowly, he unbuttoned my poor, fading duster coat down the front, slipping it around my waist. 'You're beautiful,' he groaned, probably faking it. 'What shall I say you resemble . . . a Picasso?'

I was stung, slapped across the mouth. My face wasn't those angular, broken lines with protuberant cheekbones, the long chins and eyes without depth. Shergill was surely what he should have said. Gauguin even. Moments later, I had vanquished the injury. He was a soldier, wasn't he? And not expected to know painting on top of everything else.

We lay now, kissing with eagerness each other's neck and shoulders and breast. I felt something press upon my stomach, unyielding, urgent, something I had read about, but which seemed in no way threatening or remarkable.

'I want to hear you say my name,' he murmured.

'Nilu, Nilu. I've wanted to say it aloud so many years. Nilu.'

He moved against me then, how he moved, kissing me,

holding me so tight my breath came in gasps, and his body was upon me, heavy as a tree ... I thought once I should die. Then he was still, and on my stomach stood a wetness that spread, that adhered. I felt it would be wrong to wash it off. He kissed my eyelids and held me a long time. Finally, before going downstairs, I asked:

'Before you leave, will you wake me up?' Nilu was to catch the train for Lucknow at daybreak.

He nodded: 'And how I shall miss you.'

When I awoke next morning, Nilu had already left several hours ago. Mami had seen him off. In the days that followed, I wrote the poetry and British history papers with the alertness of a fly locked in a cloud of DDT and, with my head still an iridescent blur, I left a week later for Benares.

CHAPTER THIRTEEN

Damyanti had brought Beni Madho a cup of tea as he was dressing for work that morning. She had stumbled over the doorstep, and before she knew it, there it was, the tea on Beni Madho's cracked, dusty sandals and him swearing softly, examining his white dhoti for stains. He called her luckless, a curse upon the household. Another time, she would have clenched and unclenched her fist, and lurched hopelessly away in the direction of the kitchen. Beni Madho looked up to find his wife watching him with a small smile. Was she going slowly mad? Woman abandoned by Lakshmi, he said aloud. She tried to recompose her expression into a less offending one, but there sat Beni Madho looking like a large ruffled hen (in an easy chair), scratching the dirt, unable to lay its egg. He stood up later with a small cluck, his arms in fleshy arcs beside his large body, and as he departed, his wife was smiling again at the distrait white fowl that had failed to deliver and, hopping up in impatience, had strutted away.

Now, as she slipped the taanpura into its silken shroud, the strains of the jaunpuri were in her ears:

> *Chchom chchun-a-nun-a, chchom goes my anklet,*
> *Telling me my love is on his way.*

There's something strange in the air, thought Damyanti, for none of the old thoughts comes to me any more. I used to think, maybe he'll touch my wrist as I serve him lunch, and not go out to other women in the afternoon. All those years, it seemed to her, she had always been after some-body's attention, her mother's, Beni Madho's, even that of her mother-in-law. When Beni Madho had first insulted her, called her a barren well, she had laid her head in Amma's lap to dull the throbbing. 'Men do things like that,' her mother had said. 'One mustn't pay too much attention. Besides, as they get older, they inevitably come round.' Slowly, as her mother's house filled with grand-children, their tugs and shrill cries, the physical frets of Amma's advancing age, Damyanti had found less and less to say to her. Then her mother-in-law, who had taught Damyanti to recognize Beni Madho's changing moods ('He's irritable from eating chick peas last night, they give him indigestion' or 'He's laughing because he thinks men who dance are effeminate'), died. She had taught her son's wife how to put out rows of baris in the sun with expert flicks of the wrist, and what seasoning went with different vegetables. 'Actually, I shouldn't be telling you at all,' she had said. 'When a woman eats, her nose just knows what went into the cooking.' Damyanti was beside herself, seeing the woman, who had calmly tidied her clothes and prayer books the night before, showing Damyanti where she hid her valuables, lie all at once uncaring on the verandah, her eyes shut, smiling a secret smile.

And finally, Beni Madho had graduated from the particulars of tenderest sensuality with his wife to the stealthy, coarsening explorations of the flesh elsewhere. Men are like that, said Urmila, Damyanti's neighbour, who, after nights of marital rape as a bride, had taken on the permanent staring eyes of a fish, the downward-drooping mouth ... The first time Beni Madho went to another woman, he had returned to his wife tender and full of contrition, and taken her to see a film. Damyanti had sat before the giant shapes on the screen, embracing or sparring with one another, full of suspicious wonder at her husband's solicitude. On the second occasion, he had been awash once again with a sick-sweet repentance, and made love to his wife over and over. But something in the small, lingering touch of his fingers, the uncertain fumbling in known nooks, told her he was making love to another woman. She moved away, stung. Beni Madho laughed first, and reached out to gather up the comely bounty of his wife into his arms, but Damyanti picked up her hard little pillow and, eluding further fumblings, left to sleep on a mat in the verandah. Afterwards, whenever her husband came home with his hair too neat or smelling of a strange hair oil, Damyanti recoiled in a deep physical disgust. For over a year, she alternated between revulsion for a man who had wounded her in the only part she had opened out to him, her sex, and day-long fits of weeping: she saw her life ended before it had even got off to a start. Sometimes, out of nowhere, hope (eternal enemy of the sentimentalist) would spring up; he'll give up these women when he finds out their real judging thoughts, no loyalty to anybody; he'll come back and beg for forgiveness. Beni Madho never found out, which is to say, he never changed, and began instead to take his pleasure abroad with a greater assertiveness and arrogance. He had arrived at last at the door of unending pleasure. Or so it seemed at the time.

Damyanti meanwhile sank into a torpor, which made even moving around the house a task. She ate a lot of scraps, sitting in one place, then moved to small activities, cleaning the rice, soaping her clothes, for hours at a time, keeping her mind firmly anchored to the gleam of a vessel, the weight of the grain, the weft of a cloth. What pleased now was the predictable – the milkman at five, a bath with soap and oil at twelve, and the dwindling twitter of sparrows in the dusk. It was a bit like music practice, where you sang the notes in the same sequence over and over. The difference with life was that the sequences came minus the focus or charge of music-making, they came minus the final beat, the sam. One day, she would get it right ... Beni Madho, for whom the world was still rich with stimulation, settled meanwhile for derision and silence as the most stable responses to his wife. I need to escape from the damp, smelling weight of my marriage, he told himself, my wife who gave me no child, who never laughs or lays a claim to all my attention even when I'm home. One has to survive ... I've things on my mind, male things that grab you and moisten the pores, not the life insurance and annual increment my dull neighbours live and die for.

Damyanti no longer felt sure of what would make her happy now, indeed of who she really was, if somebody were to ask. An irascible schoolmaster's adoring wife, who longed for her husband to be always by her side? Slowly she would have shaken her head, it wasn't so interesting any more, a man's tantrums and attention, even his praise. When Beni Madho growled these days, what had once been the thin skin of a quietly eager bride was still surprised, but the scabs of affront, the shying, soon fell away – became an irrelevance, the residue of an emotional habit of years. And as she grew less attentive, the tightness about her temples and mouth fell away, leaving her quiet with the security of one who has little left to lose.

She felt these days that she was waiting all the time for something she had to do. In the dark at night, there would run through her brain a faint and beautiful tune in the raga bhim palaasi, the notes growing in power, turning this way and that, changing speed or combinations, till Damyanti nearly sang out aloud. But she had to wait till it was morning, and Beni Madho had gone to school, when she would settle for some hours, doing first voice exercises and then dredging up from the dim pond of her curious childhood song after sensuous song in a poetic Bhojpuri.

In the early days, when she neglected to do the dishes in the morning, the lodger could be heard groaning and making sucking sounds with his teeth in the kitchen, as he washed the tea things lying about in the sink before rushing off for morning class.

In the evenings, she would wait once again for Beni Madho to leave the house. (Isn't he dressed yet, she'd ask herself, keeping an eye on the bedroom door. It's nearing eight, you'd think there was no one left to visit in this town.) For the deep, rich notes of the evening raga, durga, would be gaining ground in her consciousness, along with the thirst, the dull passion the musical are said to have in place of feelings, which treads with them ceaselessly through the day. It could just as well have been the raga charukesi, on the other hand, that she heard Ravi Shankar declare he had invented the other night on the radio. Invented, she had scornfully said to the lodger, sitting on a mat beside her, the Madrasis would have known it long before us. At other times, when Ashwin was home early, he would bring his radio down to the courtyard so she could listen to the old 78s of Kesarbai and Abdul Karim Khan that an inspired lunatic at the local station had taken to repeating on alternate nights.

Is it something the boy has said, wondered Damyanti, that makes me like this, dull in my feelings, and suddenly displaced in Beni Madho's throbbing world. She couldn't remember. What I do know, she thought with certain warmth, is that if he hadn't come along to torment me the way he does, I'd have slipped long ago into the land of the tongueless, living dead.

CHAPTER FOURTEEN

At the top of the steps, framed by Ujala's door, stood Beni Madho, looking out on to a darkening street. It was after three in the afternoon (with gauzy black clouds scudding across the sky's heaving breast), and the woman was not yet back from dancing class. She left at ten each morning, coming home, it seemed to him, later and later each day. Can one dance five hours at a stretch, wondered Beni Madho glumly, without an exchange of confidences or . . . needless touching, at some point. Maybe she took refreshments with the guru after rehearsals, maybe worse. Beni Madho had arrived at the teacher's house one afternoon (inflamed with thoughts of Ujala's soft neck, her long, dark trunk) to take the young woman home. Her face blackened when she saw him. She had thrust his hand away and walked the distance in silence, flashing the whites of her eyes.

'Guruji doesn't like it, you understand?' she spat as they reached her house. 'His concentration is like a flame, and he demands the same of his pupils. If I see you lurking once more around his house, you can get out of my life. Scram, you understand, for good.' With that, she had firmly shut her rickety front door, which had once been a packing case for a refrigerator, the fangs of a black-painted address still showing dimly through the green paint.

So Beni Madho waited meekly, helplessly upon her doorstep, unmindful of his father's name, the unkind mirth of the eyes that beheld him there, a man without a woman. He felt a few drops of rain spray his hair, nose and eyelashes, then stop abruptly. Already, the shops about had begun to rally with lights against an early night, looking romantic and unreal, the sets of a Raj Kapoor film from the 'fifties. You felt that any minute now, a cadaverous youth with a red kerchief and paan-stained mouth would strike up the sharp chords of a harmonium on his hip. And any moment, a beautiful young woman in ghagra and choli would pout, toss a petulant plait, and beat a twinkling rhythm upon the pavement with her anklet. But that was make-believe, thought Beni Madho with a sigh, the only place where pleasant things happened nowadays ... From across the street emerged a face and body that he knew, knew too well, and he ducked behind the door. Damyanti. What was she doing walking about before the shops like a grand lady, overweight, chewing paan, a bead-studded bag over her arm? Hadn't he left her cleaning the kitchen less than an hour ago?

There were more surprises in store for Beni Madho that afternoon. Close behind his wife loped a slender young man with a ludicrous paper mask over his face, one of those striped yellow-orange affairs that was neither cat nor tiger, leering obscenely at passers-by. Three ragged children danced beside him. It was the lodger ... Damyanti stopped before some household plastics being sold on the pavement. She picked up two buckets, a red and a white, haggling gently with the shopkeeper, and handed them to tiger-face to hold. Just like that, without a look or word of contrition, she gave the lecturer just-back-from-England her burden of inessentials to carry. The children now came up to Ashwin, wanting to touch the plastic buckets. Two dipped their thin, muddy arms into the red one and glanced wildly about them, as if by a trick, a miracle, fate's inexplicable quixotry, they would come up today with a treasure.

A young woman in chooridar-kameez and cropped hair stood watching this group with amusement. She came up then and said something to the lodger. The mask came off, he appeared to be giving directions. He also laughed a little, running tidying fingers through his long, dark hair. Young men today didn't believe in looking smart, or pleasing the women in any sense, thought Beni Madho. The lost-looking girl with knitted eyebrows walked away quickly, with Ashwin craning his neck to keep her in view for a while. Then Damyanti came up and put some guavas she'd bought into a bucket, unaware of a seething Beni Madho across the street. She looked free and content in a way that he had never noticed before. As if she had let something go, and there was nothing any more over which she could be bothered to lose her sleep. Slowly, she and the lodger walked home.

Two evenings ago, Beni Madho had stood at the Chaur-asia paan shop with his friends, a radio blaring with a whooping yahoo number from *Junglee*, with which Shammi Kapoor had jived his peristaltic way into the hearts of the peanut-popping masses. There rose from the vicinity a fragrance of marigold as somebody sprinkled a basketful of orange garlands with water, and Abdul Rafiq (who ran a tailor's shop) watched Beni Madho's hooded eyes dart once again to Ujala's small, sooty window. Had

128

the lights come on, the curtains been parted to let in the eager evening, any music yet?

'Panditji,' he said, 'you've cut the tongue out of our mouths. And brought shame upon your grey hairs for a two-takaa bit when a diamond languishes in your home.' You should talk, thought Beni Madho, with two wives tearing at each other's thin plaits in their ill-lit, rat-ridden zenana. He smiled at Rafiq as if to say, we're men of the world, you and I, with needs the kitchen stove at home won't satisfy. Our trouble is we make no secret of our doings.

'Well said, Rafiq mian, well said,' applauded Saxena the lawyer, his snout full of paan. 'People's mouths fell open when Misra first brought his bride to Allahabad. That was years ago, but with her comeliness and thrift, her patience, that Brahmin girl could have nabbed a bigger fish than our Beni Madho.'

The schoolteacher snorted. The fellows sounded as if they'd never been married ... where was the poetry in domestic routine? Could each be blind to his wife's thickening neck and its little furrows, the drowning dull-ness of her concerns? But getting into an argument with these fellows meant being late ... They didn't understand love, did they? It only happened to a few, the lucky ones. It was a bad idea letting men speak openly to you about your wife, in any case. They'd give advice, and before you knew it, they'd be asking to make her acquaintance.

Ujala's window was ablaze now with the light from two hundred-watt bulbs, drawing Beni Madho, a giant fluttering moth, irresistibly away from his friends. 'He'll get his paan from a soft hand tonight,' said the paan-seller, his own a deep red right up to the wrist. 'The quality of leaf and tobacco are of no account.'

Once Beni Madho too had found Damyanti beautiful, the chiselled nose, and eyes that briefly shut every time you raised your voice. In the beginning, as she sewed, cooked or mopped the floor, Damyanti had sung all over the house, but he soon stopped that. Bapu upstairs liked quiet. Besides, it wouldn't do to have the neighbours hear a schoolmaster's wife sing plangent ditties of love while he was away. After the third year, when she still bore him no child, the singing altogether ceased. Which was all right since he had hardly looked for a leading vocalist in his wife. What did one say to a woman who noticed neither elections nor sport, nor indeed anything about the world (a poem, a politician, economic trends) unless she could connect it with her own life? That was the other thing he disliked, Damyanti turning her face away as if he'd struck her, every time Beni Madho told the truth. About her childlessness or being fat. He hated her meekness. Beni Madho would have liked a wife who laughed loudly and disobeyed him, who interfered in all he did and ordered him about. In his head, he saw a vision of himself eagerly kneading a woman's lower back or feeding her with his hands ... Damyanti demanded nothing. She quietly darned her old saris, letting out the seams of her faded blouses till her mother sent new ones. When Beni Madho came home in the evenings, she seemed to be trying to fade into the wall, as if it was *her* fault that she existed. Beni Madho would have liked a woman to demand an explanation, even throw things at him, so they could scream and cavil and finally embrace over his misdemeanours. The way Ujala did ... but there was no one quite like Ujala, that volatile, changeable hind who had him so firmly in her power. She let him make love to her once a week, he never knew which day it would be, and the other six days she spent laughing cruelly at him.

CHAPTER FIFTEEN

In Benares, at my father's house, Sujit and I ungratefully ate and slept and resisted mutely all demands made on us to share in the responsibilities of the home, the family business, even of meeting the local people. Which is not to say we lacked feeling. We lacked only the routine imposed by normal parents to induce order into the chaos that constitutes (at a certain age) their offspring's personal lives. It had a connection with the hospital, built as it was uncomfortably close to the house, thrusting life (and its opposite) continually up against our resisting noses. But because of which the timetables and the sweet rhythm on which other homes are built, and which Ratna still tried (whining and fitfully) to insinuate into our lives, came hopelessly unstuck. Packed away into the back drawer before even half the day was over, as the charming luxury which would have to wait for its time.

The operating theatre came alive with activity at seven every morning, throwing the kitchen at home into a tizzy over breakfast for the visiting doctors. I would awaken around eleven after a night of glorious reading and listen to stories of the outdoor patients arriving at all hours with their families to cook and sleep and defecate in the hospital compound till it was their turn to be examined. Ratna ran the hospital energetically, taking time off to scold the mali at home (he was a village dancer in private, who coiled and uncoiled whole mornings for our delight, forgetting to dig up the front lawn for the monsoon). To instruct the cook (unbearably close to lunchtime) and address a series of tantrums to Sujit and me for our indifference to baths, morality or her friends, whichever was uppermost in her mind. Somewhere through her running footsteps and proclamations of small disaster, it hung together, the home and family livelihood, like a huge patchwork quilt, with fresh whims and spangles sewn on every day, keeping the family fed and warm for the night ... I let the world rush frenziedly about, earning its livelihood and its fame, while I drank cold coffee to the sounds of Ravi Shankar playing the asavari in vilambit laya, the late morning raga of yearning.

Sujit was in Benares, ostensibly studying for his pre-medical tests at the time. He had many friends, which came as a surprise since he had in no wise departed from the laconic speech of his childhood. There was a feverish interest in girls now, and in the mornings, Sujit rubbed Vaseline on his chest before the mirror, urging the few hairs about it to grow. I barely saw him since he was out at all hours, driving at maniac speeds around the city, eating spicy meats with friends, laughing in the way he had (embarrassed, under his breath) at other boys' tales of unsuccess with women. He was seeing three girls himself at the time with an equal ardour, at different spots, surreptitiously, the only way Benares allowed. One of their fathers, a policeman, got wind of his doings and came looking for Sujit in a cinema hall one afternoon, with blood on his mind. Sujit fled the city, and didn't return for two weeks afterwards.

Our house was on the city's outskirts, and in the

evenings I walked up and down the terrace, waiting for an orange sky to dim to dusk, when light from pale orange lanterns would start up in the dark, thatched village huts around. Through the roofs rose woodsmoke from fires below slow-cooking broths, as a herd of silent, chewing cattle came without haste through dust to their watered yard. Sometimes it rained a warm rain and I stood drenched to a layer beneath the skin, turning over in my head — with repeats in the parts that caused shivers — scenes with the new-found Nilu, his firm embrace. Till Ratna called me in.

We had three black labradors that spent the evenings frightening visitors, racing each other up the drive or wrestling furiously on the lawns. One evening, all three gathered on the porch and set up a low, sickening howl for nearly an hour that no threats from the servants would silence. Around two in the night, when all was quiet, the gates clanged and four men brought in a very sick man from a nearby village. He neither tossed nor groaned but lay there with his eyes closed, sweating gently on the cool verandah. Sujit was up first beside the villagers, chewing his lower lip, cracking his knuckles, in an agony for Biren to awaken and come out of the door. His father, who would kneel beside the man with his brisk, unsentimental listening, tilting the eyelid and body, holding delicately a sapless wrist. You should have left home earlier, my good men, he would finally say in a voice louder, more matter-of-fact, than his own. This man is no more. Swiftly then, he would return to bed, rubbing his nose and cheeks with rough, circular strokes, to read an article by Khushwant Singh. (Biren liked Khushwant Singh, his irreverence and elegant prose, the breathless, grunting ribaldry of his generation.) Sujit and I both lay awake for hours afterwards, clenching our fists, crazed by the light froth beside the man's mouth, that nothing, nothing could be done for him. There were no tears or ululations from the villagers at that hour, just a final, sleepless despair as they walked in silent file out of the gate.

One morning, there was a letter from Sreela, Bela's married sister, to say she was coming to visit us in Benares with her husband and children. And her brother, Nilu Haldar. I thought again of a hot summer night, of warmth in our faces and chests, and being swallowed inch by terrifying inch by a black crêpe sky webbed with tiny stars. I'll come to Benares, he had said, breaking a small silence, just you wait ... Ratna and Biren were pleased, the rush and tedium of their every day threatened with a glamorous interruption they had missed for many years. They got the bigger chores out of the way, and scheduled a dinner party for the arrival of the guests.

Things were going grievously wrong in the subcontinent, meanwhile, with bad tidings from across the eastern border. We heard (mainly from newspapers) of East Pakistan's stark poverty, and brutal atrocities against its people of late by soldiers from the Punjab. The plunder of villages, intellectuals being murdered ... The populous, river-run country was said to be organizing in revolt, village by village, against the rule of West Pakistan. What we saw was hundreds and thousands of the poor from the east invade and sweep across India like a swarm of stricken locusts. They brought as part of their baggage an epidemic of sore eyes, which crossed the northern states of India in waves. It was called Joi Bangla, victory to the Bengali. For some of us, it spelt disaster ... About this time, I had come to ponder the meetings that brought Nilu to Allahabad again and again. He planned operations, he said, for the eastern sector. What military 'operations' could there be in peacetime? Why in the east? The news from Bangladesh now began to leave a train of clues which broke through even my natural numbness to larger events. The day before the arrival of the guests, Biren, Sujit and I began to rub horribly our veiny, red eyes that were giving out a revolting white trickle. Conjunctivitis. I applied ointment and started to drug myself hourly with antibiotic, but when they finally came, the three of us stood smiling wanly from a distance, purblind inside sunglasses. For days, I didn't go anywhere near Nilu (or even speak properly to him) from the humiliation, till one evening he stopped me in one of the bedrooms:

'I can't stand it,' he said. 'I come all the way, I take all sorts of risks, and in your own home you won't speak to me.'

'You wanted to come,' I replied, struggling to hide the redness, dabbing steadily at my eyes with a handkerchief.

'God knows, I've looked forward to seeing you,' he murmured, clasping my shoulder, bringing his face up close.

'Don't,' I fought. 'You'll get conjunctivitis.'

'So I will,' he replied, and kissed me firmly on the mouth. I too had thought about his coming, his gentle need, and outside was the summer rain, the crickets, and when the rain momentarily stopped, glow-worms. I kissed his hands and the beautiful creases around his eyes.

In the mornings, I still slept late and ate my lazy, musical breakfasts with an addiction, but in the afternoons, with the family either asleep or scattered across the city by its chores, Nilu and I would dance quietly in the sitting room to Henry Mancini's alluring treacle. We often kissed behind the doors of the guest room, but that summer was mainly long evenings at table with the others, where through all the gruesome family jokes and cheerful personal slander, the secret of our bond hung for both of us like fragrance or a favourite old-world tune, giving all the inanities around a heartbreaking significance.

In the night, Sujit and Nilu slept on camp beds on the first floor terrace. I would steal up the stairs around one and pinch Nilu awake, so we could stand against a wall, whispering to each other beneath layers of whirling, black cloud. He said one night that he loved me. He also said: 'I don't have a gift this time, but when we meet again, I would like to get you something that you like.' (Actually, on the day of his arrival, he had handed me a giant bottle of cologne, Four-seven-eleven, that I'd been fiddling with among his things.)

'Maybe I can have a child from you,' I offered with the unthinking temerity of youth.

'A child,' he gasped. 'Do you know what you're saying? Here I haven't even . . . made love to you. You're very young, and will want to marry somebody one day. I was anxious that you should come to no harm . . . believe me, it was difficult that night in Allahabad. Do you understand how I love you?'

I nodded. 'Maybe I could have the baby from you *after* I am married?'

'Let me see what I can give you for your wedding,' he replied, clipping my fancy in its reckless flight.

'I want a diamond nose stud, a real sparkler,' I said, 'the kind Begum Akhtar wears.' I was singing her ghazals in those days with a sedulous accomplishment.

'So you shall have,' he whispered, 'a diamond for your

136

neat little nose. About the other thing, we need to think a little harder. You may not love me then.'

That would never be, I wanted to say, for in those days love was for ever, but the rain came, and in a moment washed off the wet shapes his lips were making on my cheek. I went downstairs.

One day, Maya Wilson, a quiet girl from college with hair down to the knees, came to spend the afternoon. Nilu danced with her for over an hour, looking deep into her eyes, and speaking eagerly in the lowest tones. I could have been the carved wooden screen at the room's edge for all the notice the two took of me. It occurred to me that intimacy for this elegant man was a habit, a character trait that had alighted upon me purely by accident. Perhaps there would be many such accidents ... For two days afterwards, in search of something that would not betray me, I avoided Nilu, reading, playing with the children, careful always to be polite to him. Then came the lunatic dinner party Biren had planned, with ninety guests strolling about the terrace like spirits in search of a body, huge cauldrons and spits with long kebabs turning brown, turning black, and ice cream melting on knolls of mango. In the library upstairs, somebody was showing a film, something surgical, with lots of bleeding viscera freely on view ... I was not yet dressed for the evening, and stood before my bedroom cupboard, looking for a blouse, unclad above the waist. In the distance, a door opened, giving me a start. I think I must have screamed a little. He put the latch up then, and stood leaning against the wall a long time. Finally, he walked up to me and removed the sari gently from my shoulder, divesting me as he would a tearful child of an expensive caprice. Softly, he kissed my sulking breasts.

'I forgive you,' said Nilu, 'but don't ever stop talking to me again. I thought I would go mad in the last twenty-four hours. Do you promise?' Maya Wilson, I felt sure, hadn't seen those darkening irises, the longing in them, the frightened love.

Soon it was time to leave for Allahabad and the final year of my MA. We sat one evening (Ratna, Sreela and her family, Nilu and I), drinking tea in the living room, and eating slightly overdone spinach pakoras. Nilu hardly spoke but watched me more than usual, smiling now and again with a complicity that he should have avoided. The pakoras fell short. I was preparing to go without when Nilu passed his plate to me. Too much eating around here, he said, don't show me food again. Ratna's instincts had been giving her clues for some days that pleased her not at all. She watched Nilu now with a loss of humour ... Once, many summers ago, when he still came to the family on annual leave, Nilu had had eyes only for her. He had stilled her anxieties, watching her skin go pink as he listened to her good-natured gripings with a tender, unconditional assent.

'Have you finished packing?' asked Ratna suddenly, twisting a resentful neck in my direction. 'Shouldn't you go and do it now?' My train was to leave the following night.

I'd been laughing (a little hysterically) with Sreela over something Sachi-mama, her father, had recently failed to do, his genius for irresponsibility. 'Oh, packing,' I said, clumsy and failing to connect. 'I can do that tomorrow morning.'

'Tomorrow will be too late. You realize what time she wakes up?' Ratna looked at Nilu, a dangerous bell in her voice, the peremptory table variety. 'Eleven o'clock!' The faces around her failed to register the disapproval she had counted on.

'But I've only a few clothes and books to put away. Take me an hour. Why are you getting so worried?'

'"Why are you getting worried?"' mimicked Ratna, high-pitched and furious. 'Is that any time to wake up ... eleven in the morning, with half the day already gone? If you had the least bit of interest in this household, you wouldn't be able to lie all morning with a sheet over your face.'

'What am I supposed to do?' I mumbled.

'Never mind, boudi,' mediated Nilu. 'Don't get so angry. She's home for holidays after all.'

'Why, we'd all of us lie in,' offered Sreela, pouring what she thought was oil, 'if we just had half a chance.'

Ratna began to rant, first tearfully, then with increasing fury. 'Here I'm trying to tell her what's right, to change her ways, and all of you go siding with her. As if I'm the one in the wrong. A wonderful thing, isn't it, sleeping your days away?' The beautiful young man in her house ... so polite, but with his attention slipping, turning, shifting its focus irretrievably away from her. Everybody was defending her daughter. 'What, I would like to know, is my position in this house if all that I say will be contradicted instantly? But go on, all of you, take up for her.'

Sreela signalled me to leave the room. I went.

We had dinner that night at the Benares club, an open-air event preceded by a variety show by infantile, rich women trussed up as rustic males in dhotis or telling tasteless jokes about spineless husbands ... I wore a black cotton sari with a thin pink border, and I felt I must be beautiful with Nilu staring at me across the lawns.

By eleven thirty, we were home again. I had just entered the bedroom and stood wearily before a heap of clothes upon the bed, when Sujit came in and shut the door.

'What have you been saying to Ma this evening?' he demanded, gritting his teeth. He'd been out with his friends at teatime.

What's this about, I thought, I've said nothing, but Sujit's asking made the hackles rise. 'Whatever I said, I don't owe you an explanation.'

'You'll bloody well tell me,' he whispered from a difficulty with breathing, his face and knuckles white. 'What did you say to make Ma cry? Because the next time you open it to upset her in this way, I'll break every tooth in your mouth. Remember what I said.'

The door flew open. Ratna.

'What are you doing here?' she demanded of Sujit. 'What's he carrying on about?' She turned to me, knowing exactly what. Sujit began his piece again, released from shyness by a dash of emboldening rum and water with his friends. 'You're talking rot,' said Ratna sharply to him. 'Mind your own business, and get back to your own room. At once.'

I awoke at eleven next morning. I didn't have to try, a clock in my body made me. There wasn't that much to get up for, in any case. Briskly, I packed my saris, kurtas, books, shoes, and felt good that I had a place to go to . . . Since Nilu was busy with Sujit and Biren, I spoke to almost nobody all morning. It was lucky that nobody else felt like speaking to me either.

After dinner, before we left for the railway station, I was in the bathroom, brushing my teeth, when Ratna entered to hand me some last things, shampoo, towels, safety pins. She had thought of everything.

'I'm sorry for what happened, Megha,' she quickly said, and I saw her nose go red in the bathroom mirror. 'I apologize for last evening.'

'I'm sorry too,' I replied, my back to her. They'd taught us charity at convent school.

An episode where each person's lines had been fully spoken and, typically of Ratna, civilized and full of Christian feeling in the end. It wasn't a house to which I wanted to come back. Home was a violent place, where, from their own anxieties, somebody inevitably got into a rage and went for you, where the gouging came with a chisel and small hammer, making its way deep inside soft stone. On each occasion, I never fully understood why, what I had done ... but then I was never very good at understanding anything. Least of all that which affected my happiness.

Back in Allahabad, I went for a last drive with Nilu towards Manauri, the air force base outside the city. It had rained all afternoon, and a weak sun now struggled out of a colourless sky to pink our faces in the parked Fiat. Nilu's jaw looked heavy, his middle thickening beyond all doubt past the tautness, the slenderness, of my earliest memories. At thirty-three, there were creases around the eyes that had nothing to do with sleeplessness or fatigue. He was also the gentlest person that I have ever known.

I spoke then, struggling to gather up into the afternoon the fast-slipping threads of our circumstance. 'You said you have orders to proceed on a posting. Where is that to be?'

He was silent at first, the lingering menace of his profession between us again. 'I mayn't tell you that,' he finally said, 'but unless things change dramatically, there's going to be a war. I can't say when either, but where the war is, there shall I be ... Remember one thing, if I write to say that I'm eating the best hilsa fish in the world, we'll have reached Dacca. The Padma river has excellent hilsa and, as you know, I don't eat fish.'

I shivered. 'Will you write?'

'Yes,' he nodded, 'but to what address? I can't have my parents reading about our love.'

I gave him the addresses of Tara and Kavita at the university hostels. I loved Nilu very much at the time and didn't want him going away to any war. He could stay in Allahabad, jobless and silly, a deserter, for all I cared, but my thoughts on the subject were hazy ... Also, with a pattern that had never varied since childhood, at the end of the holidays Nilu always had to go. So he left for Lucknow once again, and I resumed my cheerful ant-life, ruled by the insensible clock of 18 Church Lane, whose untiring good sense stood branded now with a certain beauty. Where I would never allow routine to settle upon my spirit in the old way again, biting bits off in advance towards the final sleep.

CHAPTER SIXTEEN

One evening in September, when the rains had given place to a mildness, a freshness, a natural elevation of the spirit, Beni Madho entered Ujala's house. A place where they never shut the front door – it was considered ill luck – where God was the munificent visitor, to be greeted with a smile, a jest, a paan, and depending on what phase the moon was in, a visit to the inner sanctum, Ujala's room. A woman of seventy, toothless as a suckling and with many rings in her ears, met Beni Madho in the courtyard.

'She's having a bath, our young beauty,' said the woman. 'It's the night we've been waiting for.'

Then Ujala emerged from a dark bathing room (smelling childishly of Lifebuoy soap, her wet hair coiled into a red-and-white checked towel), and crossed the little courtyard to her room. 'What are you doing here?' she pleasantly enquired.

'I'd come over to say Id Mubarak ho to Abdul Rafiq,' replied Beni Madho, 'but his home is swarming with relatives, and relatives of relatives. Not an inch of space you can sit down in at his place, so I thought I'd look you up instead.'

Beni Madho entered her room and, with the ease of

an old favourite, stretched himself out on an armchair beside the bed. Ujala first wiped her hair and then (wordlessly, with absorption) proceeded to paint her toenails a gleaming crimson, fanning them afterwards with a film magazine. In a moment, she was powdering her face with a heavy pink powder, and drawing a thick, deft line of kaajal below the eyes. A beauty spot was added to her neat, cleft chin (to rob the evil eye of its power), a many-coloured bindi, and there she stood, a woman born to stoke the wonderment, the longing, of some ardent man. She's so lovely without all that muck, thought Beni Madho, watching her clack red-and-white paste bangles on to her arm. When, in the end, she sat with glistening lips and eyes upon the floor, fastening silver anklets, he ventured to remark:

'I thought it was your day off.'

'It is,' she replied, with a giggle, 'can't you see? I haven't danced all day and it's "No, huzoor" to every customer.' She dreamily stroked a deep blue organza sari that hung from the bedstead, unconscious of Beni Madho, excluding him.

'Come to the cinema,' he said, with an ache of foreboding. 'The night show. There's Rajesh Khanna acting in *Kati Patang* at the Sangam. Each of the songs is a hit. We could eat at Chajju's dhaba before we go.'

'You go see the film,' she replied, a little too quickly. 'I've things to do.' The klaxon of a big car, a Ford, sounded outside. Ujala ran to the window, and peered over the curtain's grubby frill.

'What things?' asked Beni Madho mildly. In some things, you had to take it slowly. You had no luck if you pushed. When she didn't reply, 'What's your irada,' he said, 'your plan for tonight?'

'We don't like talking,' she giggled, placing a long,

brown finger on her lips. 'Sssh. Chapp-chapp our lips go all the time. Silence is sweet.'

'And what else do you like?' said Beni Madho, nasty, sweating a little, his resolutions of patience evaporating fast. Another motor car had passed, massive, self-important, scattering Katra's vendors and cyclists with a quiet scorn. Once again, she had sprung up like a pet hound from where she sat, and glanced expectantly at the door.

She turned to face Beni Madho, her huge black eyes glimmering. 'I like dancing and shopping for pretty clothes. Best of all, of course, I like ...' said Ujala, pointing to the bed, her hand making unmistakable undulations in the air. She burst into laughter as she spoke, showing her strong, white teeth. Another time, Beni Madho would have loved her for this and clucked, calling her meri rani, my big princess. Tonight, it upset him beyond all imaginings, the wild bobbing of her sleek brown arm.

'Let's spend some time on our own this evening,' he said evenly, abandoning caution, tempting all the gods at one go. 'I haven't seen you alone for weeks.'

'What about your pale, tongueless wife, schoolmaster? Isn't it time you took *her* to the cinema? She'll cry fat tears when the heroine is abandoned, and give you your money's worth.'

'And you, what will you do?' he shouted, stung, pain at her impudence driving in with pincers. 'Pick up your petticoats and flaunt that shameless thigh for some lecher to salivate on?'

She had to clutch her stomach, she was laughing so much now, and wipe her eyes. 'Look at him,' she said, with little wet splutters. 'Never could take competition, could he? Well, that's exactly what I intend ... to lift my petticoats as high as I can, this evening and every evening.'

'Who's coming here tonight?' asked Beni Madho more quietly, struggling to get a hold on himself.

She replied, after a moment, gently, with a sobriety to match Beni Madho's: 'It's Seth Puran Chand's youngest son. He's returned from South Africa last month, where he was being trained in the cutting of diamonds. Before that, he's lived in many countries, Dubai, America, Holland, such a gentleman.'

'Whore,' hissed Beni Madho. 'What is it that bloodless, undersized son of Puran Chand has offered you for a night, the price of a diamond?'

'Rather more,' she replied, eyes glittering, 'than you'll be able to give in a whole lifetime.'

'What, has he asked you to marry him?'

'Marry!' she said with scorn. 'People don't ask for our hands in marriage. I've my whole life to think of, besides ... I want to dance like Lachchobai. I wouldn't accept him. The seth is giving me a house in Civil Lines with creepers on the porch, and a lawn. There'll be a car, servants, even a watchman. I can dance all I want with him taking care of me.'

Tears stood in Beni Madho's eyes, he begged openly, for time was running out: 'But I love you ... more than anybody I've loved in seven lifetimes. You know there's nothing I wouldn't do ... or give up for you. Woman, take pity on a fellow.'

'Oh, when I'm a lady in a grand house, you can visit me sometimes. I don't give up my friends, do I, only from now on, the seth's son will have the first right.'

'Stop it,' he said, 'it's disgusting. I thought you'd have more pride, but after all I've done for you, have you no feeling even? I can see now that your dancing is a cover-up, a tasteless, third-rate joke. What you really are is a common slut.'

146

'Except you're in love with me,' she replied, falling back on the bed, in a paroxysm of giggles again.

'I say it still isn't too late,' said Beni Madho with urgency, choking a little on his words. 'Don't go to that man. He'll use you, and when he's done, throw you out with the trash one night. Stay with me, and I'll show you how it feels to be loved deeply, respectably, by one man all your life. I'll even marry you, if that's what you want . . . Listen, listen to me!'

A gleaming silver Mercedes that neither heard had snaked up through noisy, ramshackle Katra market, and there he leaned against the door now, Puran Chand's slender son with his well-nourished skin (in silk kurta, dhoti and diamond studs), listening to Beni Madho's words with a polite attention. Ujala saw him first and came forward, a shy pleasure irradiating her face.

'You've come at last,' she said. 'I'm ready, I won't be a minute now. Won't you sit here and have a paan? Arre, mausi,' she called out to the toothless woman dozing outside, 'won't you give our visitor something to drink?' She grabbed the blue organza and entered an enclosure to dress.

Beni Madho looked up, defeated, drops of perspiration gathering on his lip, at Puran Chand's son, who smiled upon him, civilly, with an unmasked sympathy. He looked cool and untouched by foetid emotion, his snowy handkerchief brushed with a French cologne. It cut Beni Madho to the quick. Numbly, he drew on his slippers and, blinded by tears, stumbled through the back door into a black and palpitant night, rent by the knife of cleaving knowledge.

147

CHAPTER SEVENTEEN

Three days a week, for several months in Allahabad, Tara handed me letters written in a green ink, conveying, through a careful, round-lettered precision, longing and uncertainty in blue inland forms:

'My love, at work and with my children, on weekends or when I am practising strokes at golf, always I think of you. I keep trying to locate the moment when I first started feeling this way, but I cannot for it goes back a long time . . .'

I wrote: 'Even as a child, I suspected your half-closed eyes, the way your mouth curls, tentatively, demanding attention, conjuring meanings out of the big nothingness. I now understand why, after seeing you for a little while, I always had to (had to) run away.'

And he: 'I have lost, God forgive me, all desire for my wife. If I may not have you, let that be so, but I cannot want another woman. What shall I say to Monica?'

Another time, he wrote: 'In so many ways, you are still a child, open, touchy, impractical, but I must have done something good in my past to deserve the love of a person like you. I tell my older daughter the things that you say, about choosing one's friends, for example. You become the company you keep, I think you said . . . When she grows up, I have a feeling she'll understand this thing between us, maybe even get to like you. For she loves her father very much.'

I said to him: 'I lurk guiltily among the kids of my class, the folks at home, an intruder and phantom, feeling nothing of what they feel, breathing a different air. I feel like a spy, set forever apart from the ordinary by my thoughts of you. I accuse you of snatching me from my kind.'

(It was only years later that I understood I had no kind. I was an amiable spectre ranging always amidst the known and the unremarked, creatures of custom, and that Nilu – a man tired by conformity and meretricious choice – was the peg on which I most comfortably hung my separateness.)

In October, Indian troops began to move rapidly towards the borders on east and west. The indignation of the press over the bleeding of East Pakistan grew more righteous and shocked every day, it grew bellicose. A dirty cloud with bits of hissing metal was beginning to form between India and her western neighbour. The letters in green ink came not from Lucknow or Delhi any more, but from the land of censors beyond imagination's green verge, beyond time and its palpable locations, 56 APO.

'The time is here,' wrote Nilu, 'when the manoeuvres I've been trained to execute all my life will be put to the test. I want so much to show you the spot (its impossible jewel-green surround) from which I write this letter. I can't do that, but it's okay so long as the landscape keeps changing and we move, so long as I know you are in a safe place . . .'

Once he said:

'I lie whole nights in my bunker, thinking of you. It's

149

hard to visualize the years ahead, or know whether I'll be able to give you what you want from life. I do love you, my darling, with my exhausted brain, my whole hurting body, and hope that you will be very happy.'

Then war broke out with Pakistan. The letters from Nilu, though free of reference to any actual event, bred fear now, they bred a stirring disquiet. Mami, too, received a series of blue inlands in those days, and across the mine of somebody else's unspeakable danger, we exchanged frequent glances in a deep, silent sympathy. With the clamping of curfew, dark paper appeared on all the windows, and the deafening aeroplanes overhead each night must have seen only the city's bulges (the sudden tumescence of temple or mosque) as it lay drawn up (for who knew how long) in its dull shroud. In the evenings, the radio reeled off the numbers of enemy aeroplanes felled, the stations seized, forgetting always the luckless dead on both sides. The loss, the terrible loss. I wrote to Nilu more often, despairing over the uselessness of my notes on a battlefield. In late November, Suren, my father's younger brother, was reported missing at the Haji Pir pass. He was a surgeon with the army. Two cousins, lieutenants with the infantry and also fighting in the west, were taken prisoner soon after. (I carefully stored away the bottle of cologne Nilu had given me behind some books in the living-room cupboard.)

It was the sixteenth of December, with the fighting at its bloodiest since the beginning of the war. (In the morning, I had received a letter from Nilu, announcing that if he was still alive next day, there he would be, eating the best hilsa fish in the world.) The radio reported that the last seventy-two hours had brought in the heaviest casualties of the war for both sides. Through day and through night, it read out in a frightening monotone the names of people missing or dead. In the beginning, we fought to keep out of our minds the fresh, hopeful faces that had gone to the sacrifice, their mothers' destroying agony. By the evening, their numbers had crossed so many hundreds that we no longer had to try. We heard the last aeroplanes from Manauri, the air base, thundering across the night to the west, bursting our eardrums with terror. With a mortal terror.

Mami had been in the prayer room for longer than usual that evening. The rest of us sat reading in the living room till, around eight thirty, the words on my page began quietly to blur. In my brain, there took shape first a small then a bigger fright, swelling finally into a huge gobbet of panic that made me hurl my book aside. I entered the prayer room and prostrated full length before the lighted Krishna, trembling, begging with frenzy, worse than frenzy: Save Nilu's life, don't let him die. I'll do anything if you promise to protect Nilu.

The frenzy ceased. A small, calm voice with, I think, a laugh in it said: Well, yes, but can one have everything? If he lives, you mayn't get to keep him. The question is, are you ready ... to release him? He must live, I said, you have to keep him safe. It seemed the obvious choice. Clear as a bell the exchange had been, and as casual as two people blaming the weather. I dismissed it the instant I stepped out of the prayer room.

That was 16 December, or the way people under siege understand things. For those, on the other hand, who think things out, all wars come to an end and, for each war, there are survivors. On the morning of 17 December 1971, a cease-fire was announced between Pakistan and India. The war was over. That same day I accidentally broke the bottle of cologne in my cupboard, and stood stupefied before the mess of startling, over-sweet fragrance choking my books ... Relief and a power-linked elation coursed through the country's ageing veins: General Niazi had laid down his arms. To celebrate, Bela and I quickly booked tickets on a night train to Calcutta; we were going on holiday.

On the morning before we left, I received a letter written on white foolscap. It had to do with war's aftermath, and surviving, and a fateful bottle of cologne:

Dearest Megha,

This is a letter you will never expect. It turns out that Monica, my wife, was in touch with the CO right through the war. The good man said nothing to me, but dropped careful hints to the lady about certain letters I'd been receiving in the past months. Two days after the cease-fire, and completely without warning, Monica arrived at our camp, with special permission. I was away all day, so she entered my tent and read your letters. Every single one. You can imagine what happened between us when I returned. I'm sorry, little darling, I'm really sorry, but Monica's carried some back with her to India (for God knows what further nastiness).

She threatened many things. That she would kill herself, for one. I promised that I would never see you again. I told her that I loved my children more than anybody else in the world, which – incidentally – is the truth.

I shall love you to the day I die. Goodbye.

Nilu

The morning light grew thin, as if somebody was tampering with the supply, trying to turn off the beam ...

Then all went dead, the letter in my hands, the voices around, my eager youth, numb cold dead.

On another plane (where live our robot bodies that bleed and cough and change their dress, unmindful of catas‑trophe), there was no time. Within hours, I was leaving for Calcutta, where Monica Haldar waited with her family. I tried telling Bela that I couldn't travel (I was running a slight temperature) but my horrid secret made me both desperate and faint, and nobody took any notice of a word I said. Before long, I lay on a dim berth of the Kalka express, which took us at a shattering speed through the night, in the direction of Calcutta, a city I had never seen before.

The light, as we emerged at Howrah, felt harsh for a winter morning. We took a taxi that rumbled and threatened to come apart with every screech of gear, and there were many, as we proceeded at snail's pace through the city's broad streets. The driver was friendly, and informed us free of charge that Calcutta was not just rows of sooty dwellings piled one on top of another, and holes in the road, and pedestrians who yelled at motorists. It was also the home of Chuni Goswami, the singer Suchitra Mitra, and Badal Sircar, a playwright, he said in a fruity Bengali, as the cab's engine died out completely at a busy crossing. Chuni Goswami turned out to be a footballer. We had arrived in the morning rush, and passed hundreds of queuing faces atop white dhotis, each clutching a jhola and a newspaper against personal sorrow or the tedium of a working day. The big city was with us, its every sputter and clang an incitement to come alive, to claim with passion the fate of men and affairs and, no matter what, to stay that way.

Bela and I went to stay with her friend, the beautiful, dewy Noton, who lived with her mother off Gariahat. There must have been a father, at least, somewhere in the past, but as nobody spoke of him, it didn't do to ask. Noton was full of stories about a certain Ranjan-da, who lived in the house opposite, his unworldliness and changing jobs each year, his lack of humour. We saw the young swain on his terrace sometimes, thoughtfully stroking a dyspeptic stomach or smoking a quiet cigar. In later years, Noton would marry him. (Meanwhile, she just called him 'dada' or brother, as girls in Calcutta will do, and got on with dreaming about him.)

In fact, on the day of our arrival, I heard nothing of what Noton or Bela said to me. I waited in terror for the phone to ring, my ears pricked for every car that slowed down in our narrow lane. Fear rolling up into a tight little fist just below the diaphragm and, no matter what I did, refusing to go away. At last she telephoned, Nilu's wife, she'd be along within the hour ... I had the biggest of cities about me at that moment, and nowhere at all to go.

The doorbell rang. I found a dark, attractive woman with short hair, gesturing to her chauffeur with a conspicuous youthfulness. Monica was small, energetic, and giggled after every sentence she spoke. She seemed anxious to be liked.

'Megha,' she said, with instant recognition. 'I've heard a lot about you. From Nilu. He's very well up there in Dacca ... missing his children, of course. My father's arranged for him to come down on leave, a short spell ... The war can get you down.'

Bela came out to meet her then, and the house was full

of the silvery good feeling of sisters-in-law who seldom met. Monica asked us to lunch the following afternoon at her sister's house in Alipore. I have influenza, I muttered, you'll have to excuse me. Rubbish, said Bela, she'll come. She's always wanted to meet you. A car would collect us punctually next day, putting the noose more firmly about my neck.

After Monica left, there was still a beautiful winter Calcutta, the chatty, beckoning shops and clusters of people eating on the kerb. And (through fever's haze) a smell of joss sticks and vigorous young women in striped saris getting out of one clanging tram and into another. I loved the trams.

The following day, Bela, Noton and I sat dressed in pale silks, facing Monica's sister, who reclined (actually reclined) full length upon a chaise longue. She had large, round eyes in an oval face, with a lot of black make-up about the lids.

She raised herself on an elbow when she spoke, smoking a cigarette out of a jade holder.

'A small gin, darling?' asked her thin, bespectacled husband, with an expression of great good humour.

'Absolutely,' said the lady, opening wide her black-domed eyes. 'And I wouldn't make it small, if I were you.' The husband giggled nervously.

Monica was there before us, waiting for the afternoon to begin. Quite soon, two couples arrived with a lovely simultaneity, and were introduced to me. Not once to Bela or Noton, just to me. I felt their calm, appraising eyes upon my face, my movements, what evidence of class or craftiness I let fall. I waited, speechless and taut, for the next disagreeable surprise.

'You have to grant,' said Monica's sister with her generous boom-in-the-cave voice to no one in particular, 'that Brahmin girls are pretty.' Her husband giggled again. He had recently been offered a partnership in a company owned by his wife's father, a rich merchant. Noton and Bela shifted uneasily.

'Isn't Megha lovely, everybody?' said Monica then, nodding affably into the faces around. 'I think she looks exactly like Nilu.' The company burst into laughter.

'Your husband, you mean?' said the stylish sister, taking the charade forward one step. 'The gent with the big bottom and beautiful voice?'

'Thanks,' said Monica, 'I'll keep both,' accepting after brief hesitation her first gin. You never knew with people from small towns. 'Personally, I think Megha should've been born a South Indian. They marry their uncles in the south.' More laughter, only muted this time.

Bela's attention, I noted with relief, had shifted from the sitting room to lodge firmly with a groaning lunch table nearby. I cannot remember what I ate or spoke that afternoon, only the sensation of being a small, numb fly hung before some large, glittering fish that swam in slow, narrowing circles about it.

Lunch over, in the tradition of Bengali parties across the country, a couple began to sing. Rabindra sangeet with its baleful sonority, and sharp cascades of feeling. Then the sister turned her ranging searchlights upon me:

'Doesn't Megha sing? She looks artistic to me. I'm sure if we ask very nicely, Megha will give us a song?' Noton was really the musical one, who sang on the radio with a deep, trained voice, but nobody asked Noton.

'Definitely,' leaped Monica into the shallows, armed with a swift, broad knife. 'I have just the song in mind for her. Cliff Richard's *Outsider*. It's from a time when Megha was a little girl. Do you know it?' she asked, turning to me. 'Then sing.'

Out of shock and the desperate intelligence of being provender now on the enemy's warm plate, I began to sing. It wasn't my will working the vocal chords, but some irresistible power that had me impaled and keening:

> *'Someone else is in your arms tonight,*
> *While I'm all alone and blue;*
> *Someone else will kiss and hold you tight,*
> *Just the way I used to do.*
> *I used to be your love, and now I am used-to-be,*
> *Outsider, that's me.'*

A burst of clapping from Monica and her elder sister, who sat bolt upright now, from the guests an uneasy silence. They sensed at last a cold venom at work that they had come insufficiently prepared for. When coffee was served, I left the room, with Monica's eyes glinting, following me. I found a telephone in the bedroom. Sister Amy, a nun from college, was in Calcutta at the time. Stammering over faint wires, I told her where I was, of Nilu and the afternoon's gruesome event.

'What are you doing in that place, you daft creature?' scolded sister Amy. 'Leave at once or should I come and fetch you?'

'No,' I said, 'I'll manage. I'll leave.' Worked still by strings, I returned to the sitting room and asked Bela could we go home. 'Thanks for a delicious lunch,' I said to Monica's sister.

The arc lamps shone with a brief, consummatory rapture. 'It was entirely my pleasure,' she said, widening them for emphasis.

I didn't get away. From lunch, Monica drove us off to tea with her parents, two frail spectres with soft voices, with whom we sat eating rasgullas in a fragrant room.

'This is Megha,' said Monica, loudly, to her father. 'Nilu's niece. Doesn't she look exactly like him?'

'Have a rosogolla,' he said to me with a quaver, a man who had seen more highs and lows in his life than his daughter ever dreamed of. I dislike sweets in syrup, but to please him I ate one.

Then we were standing, Monica and I, at the top of a dizzying spiral staircase, with a marble chessboard hallway down below:

'You think I care,' said Monica, 'what woman my husband goes to for his amusement? But he's *my* husband, remember that. I married him, so from now on, just lay off.' Her voice was getting shrill, I was afraid that Bela would hear us.

'I give you my word,' I whispered in a terrible cowardice and despair, 'that I shall have no more to do with Nilu.'

'You better not,' she snapped. 'One wrong move, and I take those letters to all your admiring relatives in Lucknow. To your parents. I've got enough, you know. I'll make sure there's a scandal ... And don't say I didn't warn you.'

We returned to the fragrant room.

'Megha's going to eat another rosogolla,' announced Monica. 'One more, please. Just for me.' On her face sat the dazzling ingenuousness of a child, smiling, eager to please. I was going to be sick, so I shut my eyes tightly as Monica held the rasgulla up to my mouth.

Days later, Bela and I returned to Allahabad, a place no longer dispiriting or inhabited by bores. Even the parks, with their tawdry, silver-painted fences and orderly flower-beds, gave off a light, healing scent. Of cleanliness and simplicity, and people who forgave the injuries that others did to them.

CHAPTER EIGHTEEN

Damyanti had asked Ashwin to come with her to the State Bank, university branch, her second visit to the place. She had bundled the grimy banknotes into tens and hundreds, savings from a loveless marriage, and sat now on a bench, filling out (with tightly gripped pen) a close-printed form with truthful trivia. She rose then to take her place before a counter which said 'Deposits', a queue forming quickly behind her. Ashwin stood at a distance, smoking a filterless cigarette.

It was forty-five minutes after opening time. The clerk turned the leaves of a register with an expression of great patience, sipping a slow glassful of tea. He spoke in undertones to a friend sitting beside him. Fifteen minutes went by, with Damyanti's plump arm hanging its slip of paper patiently into the wall's glum rictus.

'What is it?' asked the counter clerk at last.

A tall man pushed past the waiting file and, stooping, handed some banknotes to the clerk. Damyanti withdrew her arm and turned to Ashwin with a small smile. He looked away. Another man came forward, panting slightly. He wore a pashmina shawl, and addressed the man inside with familiarity. He held out a form and his own deposit.

'Been out of town, Sethji?' said the clerk. 'You haven't been here in months.'

Again, she looked at Ashwin, confused and upset, sweating despite cold weather. The youth stared blackly at Damyanti. All he did was stub out with some violence a half-smoked cigarette into the bin beside him. Then a third man came up, good humoured and stout, except he knocked Damyanti's elbow right off the counter.

'Wait a minute, bhaisaheb,' said Damyanti, raising a palm, and bent towards the counter clerk:

'Tell me, how long are you going to ignore this queue and do everybody else's work first? If you take money from one more person before you take mine . . .'

'What's the matter?' said the clerk, looking at her for the first time. 'I'm doing my work. Who are you to tell me how I should do it? Please move on. You're blocking depositors.'

'I'm a depositor, and I'm going nowhere,' said Damyanti, quiet and stubborn, 'until you've taken my money. Quickly.'

The eyes of his friends and other customers were on the counter clerk. He did not budge. Damyanti's hand now clawed at the opening as the fat man began once more to insert his papers. The clerk stared at him.

'Why, janab,' said Damyanti, 'you haven't got far, have you? Just take this man's money and see.'

'What will you do? Who are you, anyway?' he asked, his voice grating and ugly, as if he would begin to swear any minute.

'What will I do?' Damyanti addressed the queue behind. 'He comes in late and sits there drinking tea, talking to friends, while we drop our work and travel halfway across town to stand here. Then he overlooks everybody waiting, and does whose work he pleases. I bring money to your bank, my good man. If you don't take it right away and give me a receipt, I'll see your manager. I shall close my account, and ask for your dismissal. Never mind who I am.' She shook a bit from the effort, her chest registering a small wheeze.

They began to rally, the men behind. She's been here the longest, we're all tired. This bank really makes you wait. Why don't you take her deposit? The stout man withdrew his arm. From the other counters, the clerk's friends began: 'Arre, yaar, chalo bhi, when are you going to start collections?'

Angrily, the counter clerk snatched her heap of bank-notes and the deposit slip she had filled in so gravely, pondering every line. He began to count.

Ashwin was smiling as they came out. 'You should've seen yourself,' he said. 'Eyes wide as Durga's in full battle, cheeks glowing ... For a minute, I thought you were going to hit somebody.' He laughed long and soundlessly, throwing a new packet of cigarettes up once, twice into the air ... Pride and disbelief at the antics of the groveller of Beni Madho's backyard. Again he spoke: 'You were good, you know. I'd got up to help when the argument began, to punch the fellow's nose in, if need be, but I sat down again. It was obvious you didn't need me.'

She looked into Ashwin's face, was he praising her? People made you so angry with their rudeness, their lack of feeling, what else could she have done? Damyanti snapped shut her bead handbag, light now as a cloud, and walked briskly home.

Another day, she was on her way to the railway station with Urmila, who had to buy tickets for a journey. She

161

met Ashwin drinking tea in the front room. Could he come along with them, the lodger asked.

'What for?' said Damyanti. 'Urmila and I can manage. You needn't worry,' she added, 'I shan't clamber on to the first train I get and vanish from your lives. Not yet.'

'No?' said Aswhin. 'I just wanted a walk. Please. It's such perfect weather, and I've four free periods this morning.'

At the station, with Urmila at the counter and Ashwin talking to an acquaintance somewhere, Damyanti stood beside a group of girl guides (their tents and sleeping bags and knapsacks), eavesdropping on their camping plans. Piled just behind her were a dozen black-painted, aluminium trunks, one on top of another, with the names of army jawans (Jauhar Singh, Sardool Singh) returning home from the war. It was 1972, the year of reunions, and the return of a much-desired peace.

From the inner platform rushed out a thin, middle-aged man with a lined face. He was dressed in a dusty dhoti and kurta, and wore no shoes. Without stopping to think, he dived behind the little tower of black trunks. What was he doing, thought Damyanti, playing hide-and-seek at his age? Close on his heels came two paunchy, cat-eyed policemen, tapping their pink palms with impatient batons. They addressed Damyanti:

'Have you seen a short man, bibiji, running out a moment ago? He had a red jhola hanging from his arm.'

'What's he done?' she timidly asked. Had the fellow stabbed somebody with a knife, or kidnapped a baby? It happened all the time.

'He was caught,' replied the older policeman, with the air of purging the world of crime, 'travelling without a ticket.'

'Oh,' said Damyanti, with disappointment and relief,

her brain working furiously meanwhile. Consummately, after the briefest pause, she announced: 'Yes, I saw him running that way, where the taangas are . . .'

'Are you sure?' said the younger policeman, loftily, with distaste. Accounts by the public were usually so full of holes.

'You asked me, and I told you. Hurry or he'll give you the slip.' The policemen padded away.

The ashen man emerged behind Damyanti, swooping again like an expert police-dodger on to the inner platform. Nimbly, he jumped down to the tracks, his dhoti raised, and fled in the mild sunlight towards his city and freedom.

Ashwin had watched Damyanti ever since the delinquent had secreted himself behind the trunks in her vicinity. He thought she would move away, it was only sensible, but there she stood, rooted to the spot, giving moustachioed policemen directions, if you please. He saw the emotion on her face change in a few moments from fear to pity to, finally, a faint, seeping smile of collusion.

'You're getting awfully smart, aren't you?' he said, coming up and wagging a stern finger at her. 'If the police come looking for you, I know nothing about your motives. I'll hand you over quietly so they can teach you about the law.'

One February afternoon, Damyanti sat drying her long, waving hair in the sun, knitting a Fair Isle pullover for Urmila's grandchild. From time to time she rubbed wax from a stump of candle on her tapering fingers – it kept the hands smooth in cold weather. As she looked up, she saw a young woman standing in the doorway, making no move to enter.

'Does Dr Krishna live here?' asked the girl in Hindi,

her sari revealing a pair of tennis shoes. Her hair was cut in a short crop, she could have been in her teens.

'Who?' said Damyanti.

'Dr Ashwin Krishna. 45 Colonelgunj was the address I was given. My professor has sent me to meet him.'

'Oh, Ashwin,' said the older woman. 'This is where he lives all right, except he isn't back yet from class.' The girl joined her hands, turning to leave. 'Don't go,' called Damyanti. 'On Fridays, he's usually home by a quarter past three. Won't you wait a while?' She pulled a second cane chair into the sun, and asked the girl her name.

'One of his students, are you?' said Damyanti, conversationally. 'I don't see you with the lot that comes over here.'

'No,' replied Megha. 'I'm in another department, English. He teaches history. Dr Krishna and I've been asked to do a play together, a long play, in two months' time. I wonder whether we'll make it, but I'd like to, very much.'

What Damyanti saw when she looked up between the stitches was a pale young woman who was either ill or under some kind of stress. She spoke in little jerks, pressing her knuckles to her temple, and closing her eyes from time to time.

'Are you his mother?' the girl was asking as Ashwin Krishna entered the courtyard.

She went up to him at once. 'I'm Megha Lahiri. It's about that play Professor Sahai wants us to do ... I don't know whether you've thought about it, but it's to be in three acts, and we've barely two months to go.'

'Yes,' he nodded, surprised by the intrusion. 'Sounds like short notice ... but haven't we met somewhere? At a poetry reading or concert, perhaps?'

'I don't go to any,' said Megha firmly. 'I'll tell you

where I've seen you though. One afternoon in Katra ...
It was just starting to rain. You wore a tiger mask,
something memorable.' She smiled, showing shiny white
teeth.

'I remember, yes,' he said, laughing. 'I've heard about
you from Tara and Kavita. Friends of yours, aren't they?'

She nodded. 'I've brought a couple of plays along,' she
said. 'I figured if you had the time, we could begin
reading at once.' She looked as if her life depended upon
it, the play, the getting down to it.

Ashwin was to meet two colleagues at the department
and propose certain changes to the European history
syllabus. 'I have the time,' he said, without hesitation,
lowering himself on to a wooden takhat on the verandah.

For the next hour, they spoke of plays they had read,
the difficulties of costume, where they would draw the cast
from. After some argument, they began to read *The House
of Bernarda Alba*, taking turns with the parts. Megha read
a long passage, her voice deepening and lifting with the
emotion, the pace and modulations of an actress. Perfect,
he thought, looking at her with surprise:

'You're good at this, aren't you?' said Ashwin. 'Have
you been with the theatre some time?'

She nodded. 'All the undergraduate years. It's the only
thing I can do, act ...' she said, smiling. 'I'm not very
good at life.'

He looked curiously at her face, was she saying it for
effect? Didn't sound like it, yet there were not many people
(here or in any place) who spoke that way, impulsively,
from the gut.

'Aren't you going to get your visitor some tea?'
Damyanti called out. 'You're screaming yourselves hoarse
as it is.'

Ashwin left for the kitchen.

Damyanti watched the girl sit very still, staring bleakly at some flies on the rough, cracked floor. Once, she thought, she saw her brush her eyes with the back of her hand. What could be the sorrow of one so young, so evidently well-to-do? I'm getting old, said Damyanti to herself, and suspect calamity in everything. Ashwin brought tea for all in steel glasses.

'Does vicissitude have a use?' said Megha, apropos of nothing. Once again, he thought, a revelation of her inner mind, like a pet dog laying bare its underbelly. She watched the steam rising up from the tray, making no effort to lift her glass.

'Offhand, I'd say it does,' said Ashwin to be pleasant, 'the kind you and I know. It could give us a genuine sympathy for others, and make us ask some basic questions: Is there a plan behind all this? How does one live with dignity despite suffering? Not least, of course, it gives us the poetry of Bernarda Alba . . . can you see happiness doing that?'

'But doesn't unhappiness turn people into cowards, replacing their natural generosity with ugly caution?'

'I don't know,' he slowly said, pulling at his moustache, 'I guess I'll have to live a little longer to answer that. Right now, I think it's the pusillanimous, the mean-spirited, who lose their power to give. The brave ones probably get bigger, more firm on their feet.' This is wrong, he felt, even as he said it . . . How can one speak for everybody?

They read further. After a while, Ashwin began to laugh at Indians wanting to do plays in English all the time. 'It's absurd,' he said, 'hearing those foreign sounds come out of smooth, brown faces, the botched inflexions. As for the gestures on stage, no Englishman would be caught dead moving his arms and face about the way we do.'

'You don't seem to mind using foreign words yourself in conversation,' observed Megha drily, rising to leave.

'No,' he grinned.

'That's a nice pen,' she said, pointing to the navy blue Parker he was doodling with.

'You can have it,' said Ashwin, screwing on the cap, placing his pen on the books she was beginning to gather up.

'I couldn't,' she gasped, 'it's too expensive.' What she meant was, forget it, I don't even know you.

He laughed at her discomfort. 'I've two more, if that makes it any better. Look, I'd really like you to have it.'

Suddenly, she felt tired having to argue with a stranger about why she couldn't keep his pen. She'd return it later some time. Right now, she had to get home and do the everyday things ... read, sleep, anything at all that made no demands on her deepest attention. Things like kind-ness, or a guy who could talk interestingly, were areas of danger, a cracker at Diwali that might suddenly go off in the hand. Megha left abruptly.

Ashwin sat reading some cyclostyled sheets for a while, then rose and walked slowly up the stairs. 'I know what you're thinking,' he accused an over-silent Damyanti, 'but you're wrong. She hasn't a dram of history inside her, Indian or any other.'

'She's quick,' said the matron, unusually alert. 'She'll learn. Besides, she speaks English the way you do. You're not getting any younger, you know.'

Ashwin smiled; he'd known her two years, she used to be such a mouse, now the lady was full of surprises. Damyanti knitted sternly – two plain, two purl, it was an easy patch – and thought how the girl had something about her that resembled the lodger. A lack of canniness, of calculation ... unlike Beni Madho. She lacked, that was it, the carapace the rest of us hold up to hide our weakness from the world. In the girl's case, it probably came from having had an easy childhood.

CHAPTER NINETEEN

In June the following year, with my MA behind me, I joined Ratna and Biren for a brief holiday in the hills. On our way back, we stopped at Lucknow with Ratna's parents, people I had grown up with, and who saw me more or less as an extension of their bodies. They had no choice but to love me. There were other relatives in the city who seldom noticed Sujit or me, the most notable being Kenimama, Biren's uncle, a retired insurance sales-man with an interest in Bengali theatre, who derived his sense of well-being from the acquisition of influential or rich friends. Earlier, he too had barely registered my existence. Then I went to Lucknow for my BA, and he read in the newspaper about the fancy plays (Peter Shaffer, Tennessee Williams) that my college regularly staged. Again and again, Kenimama would see the name of Biren's daughter in the reviews, the critics' praise, and the thick pores of his clever white face would tighten with spite. The girl was too much up in the air, too long spared the kitchen stove, which was a woman's proper concern. She would come to no good.

Biren, who actually liked his relatives, called on Keni-mama one evening in Lucknow. On his return, I passed him in the corridor, but found no smile or greeting on his face. He looked distracted, averting his eyes, till I became at last too distressing to ignore. 'Call your mother,' he said, hardening his voice, 'from whatever it is that she is doing.' A slim serpent of foreboding entered the dense air between us, flicking its tongue briefly as I met my father's eyes.

Then Ratna and he stood speaking in undertones in my grandmother's dressing room with its cracked floors, paandaan and lace-covered mirror. The tension was palpable, leaking into the adjacent corridor where I stood, shivering at the unbearable pauses in my parents' talk. I knew then it was here, my day of reckoning, and nothing I said or did would hold it off any longer. Not that I had many ideas. The men of the house were gathering slowly for dinner, and swiftly, without a glance in my direction, Biren strode past me to the dining room. Ratna, meanwhile, swooped to catch me in my grandmother's bedroom, with its darkness and cool camphor smell.

She didn't beat about. 'You didn't write Nilu letters during the war, did you?' she asked, hoping to trounce Kenimama's malignity once and for all.

'I did,' I replied, the hair on my neck bristling with portent, now that truth was the only course.

'What kind of letters?' said Ratna, shaken but brisk. Braced for the difficulty that stood unshakeably before her.

'They are loving letters,' I whispered, numb. 'Very loving.'

Ratna grew pale, a many-layered catastrophe upon her, fear for her daughter, public disgrace ... And proof, the sudden undeniable proof, of intimacies in the world that took away in some manner her own youth. 'Tomorrow morning, your father and I go to meet Monica, Nilu's wife. You have to come along with us ... It looks like she's taking your letters around to the relatives. Kenimama, who's always wanted something awful to happen to our family, told Biren about them today. I don't see why your father meets that wretched man. He seems to have described what you wrote to Nilu in some detail. Get your daughter married, said Kenimama, she's gone to the bad. Megha's having an affair ... You can imagine how agitated your father is.'

'Can't we skip tomorrow's visit?' I asked, my brain convulsed, but failing (as in earlier years) to own up fully to my emotion before Ratna. All the same, there it was, fear sucking sibilantly at my breath, at the bloodstream, as I stood before my mother, a slow and witless body that often caused trouble, and seldom came up with answers.

For most of the night, I burned with shame and fear, unable to picture what would really happen next morning. Surely, Monica had too much social training to let things get out of hand, make a regular scene? She had her husband after all, with no further distractions from me ...

At six, Ratna came to my bed. 'Get dressed,' she said. 'Monica's expecting us within the hour.'

It was a hot and motionless morning, with our bodies giving out tiny founts of moisture away from the fan. I wore a pale yellow sari with drooping white flowers. Nilu emerged quickly as we arrived, his eyes and nose red. He touched my parents' feet with a strange submission.

Monica came out and it turned frightening, like being suddenly in the presence of spirits. In that moment, I knew that anything, unimagined or horrible, could happen. And I stopped registering most of what the others said, the things I could have done.

'How *are* you?' said Monica to Biren. 'Nice of you to call. It's lovely seeing you again, Megha. Won't you come in?'

Biren homed in at once. 'Kenimama tells me that Megha's written Nilu some letters she shouldn't have. Is it true?'

Monica giggled, all girl, her moment before her. 'One hundred per cent,' she said. 'When I first read them, I thought I'd written them myself ... real love letters. I couldn't believe my eyes. Ask him, ask your cousin.' We stood beside decanters and a pile of coffee-table books on a carved sideboard that looked a little out of place in a white-washed government dwelling. Nilu looked away, his nose reddening again with a terrible cowardice.

'All right,' said Biren, grabbing what he gathered were the horns, 'so Megha's written these letters. I don't think she's done right, but at her age, one can make a mistake ...? When they upset you so, Monica, why didn't you come to us directly? What was the point of taking her letters to different relatives ... Somebody's getting a laugh out of all this, don't you think?'

Monica was beside herself. 'Can you imagine my shock when I found out my husband was seeing another woman? I warned her, too, that she should have no more to do with Nilu ... I can see now that she was getting her parents' support.'

Since the liberation of Bangladesh, I had made no attempt to contact Nilu. There seemed no point, for in the intervening months, the import of his last letter and the scenes at Calcutta had shot back into my head again and again, slides in a jammed projector, grotesque and streaked with pain. 'But I haven't kept up,' I stammered. Nilu was looking flustered again.

'I saw a card,' said Monica. Well, for the New Year I had sent Nilu a card, saying it's over, but it's all right. There were no hard feelings. 'Who knows,' I heard Monica keen, 'how many more your daughter sent.'

'Listen, Monica,' said Biren, closing his eyes to get the words right. As if it could all be washed away, a woman's mad unhappiness and rage, with reason's limpid oil. 'I want to tell you about these children. Megha and Sujit have grown up worshipping Nilu. If you look closely at Sujit, he walks like Nilu, he talks like him, with the same gestures. Megha's done something very wrong, but it was, how shall I say, in the nature of things. The way these children have grown up.' In my misery, I felt at once shocked and moved that Biren — through his impenetrable self-absorption down the years — had seen it all.

Monica flew into the next room, returning with a sheaf of blue, dog-eared notepaper that singed with its familiarity, and raised the room's temperature by several degrees. My fateful letters from Allahabad.

'Read them,' she said to my parents. 'Read for yourself.'

'I've left my glasses at home,' said my marvellous, humbled father, leaving to pace the featureless verandah of the army flat in anguish.

'You read them then,' ordered Monica, thrusting the crackling sheets into my mother's limp hand.

'Frankly,' said my mother in disgust, 'I'm not interested.' Into what further muddy depths of her daughter's disordered brain must she descend?

'Then I'll do the good offices,' giggled Monica, reading aloud John Donne to my mother's crumpling face:

> *'I wonder by my troth, what thou, and I*
> *Did, till we lov'd? were we not wean'd till then?*
> *But suck'd on country pleasures, childishly?'*

She read endearments and love's iridescent superlatives, goring, laying bare with the thick, bloodying needle of her voice whole realms of tenderness, the springing flesh.

She went on and on till I began to lurch soundlessly in the direction of the floor. Nilu put out a hand to steady me.

'Don't touch her!' shrieked Monica, an enraged and fearful parrot. He sprang back at once, a poor beast of conditioned reflexes.

'I think we'd better leave,' said Ratna, appealing a last time to Monica's good sense. 'I can only request you to throw those letters away.'

'You still want something from me?' hissed the colonel's wife. 'Let me tell you this. I intend to keep all the letters and take them to whoever I like, for as long as it pleases me. It'll teach a family like yours some decorum. And maybe a few decent values.'

'Don't you speak to my mother in that tone of voice,' I heard myself say. 'Or talk decorum to my family.' Nilu meanwhile kept the silence of the dead, as if he was in some other room. Surely he should have intervened, stood up for family honour. It nicked me at last, the keen surprise at ever having loved this man.

'Megha,' said my mother sharply, 'don't bother to engage with a ... person of her sort. I won't stay here a moment longer. Nilu, would you please drop us?'

Tentatively, consulting his muse, Nilu picked up the car keys from the sideboard, but Monica was instantly beside him, shrill with a new admonition: 'Put those keys where they belong. Nilu's dropping nobody, none of you. He's *my* husband.' He returned the shamed bunch quietly to a brass bowl, completing with his dull gesture a small portrait of their marriage.

'Call for a taxi then, will you?' said Ratna. Nilu left the room.

*

I locked myself afterwards into my grandmother's smoke-coloured bathroom with its wooden clothes hooks, and sat on the floor, erased and blubbering. I hoped never to come out of the door. In a while, my mother began to knock: 'Megha, your father's leaving for Benares. Yes, now. He wants to see you.' As I emerged, 'We thought you so wise,' said Ratna, 'so wonderful. To think you'd go and do something like that . . . you've let us down.' No scrap of me remained that was unpierced still or dry, or I might have cried out, yelped like a dog.

Barefoot, I walked to my father, standing beside his case in the porch. Since nothing was impossible that morning, perhaps he, too, would look stonily into my face and say . . . that I should take my trunk and go away to live in another city? Leave the family before word got around? I touched his feet, stretching, sinking, straightening up, with the numbness of a sleepwalker. As I rose, he clasped me for the first time in my memory (the blank, unending halls of my traverse) close, close to his firm, restoring breast. 'My baby girl,' he said, stroking my hair, 'my poor, thin daughter. It's going to be all right.'

In Lucknow, my mother made an appointment with an astrologer, Harishankar Trivedi, to lift, if he could, my fortunes out of the morass. A hysterical woman had called my civilized parents names, accused them of things that they knew nothing of, and I had been the cause. I went.

Trivediji was an overbearing Brahmin with a large, naked belly, who sat on a bare, raised board in a room adorned by a single calendar. He claimed to read out the course of people's destinies from a text written by the sage Bhrigu hundreds of years ago. In our state of mind, Ratna and I weren't going to be fussy.

He patted the boards beside him. 'Sit, daughter,' he ordered, addressing me with the familiar 'tu', flattening my palm with an enormous magnifying glass that had dirt around the edges. He laughed out aloud.

'Did you have to choose an uncle to fall in love with? Tell me, daughter, was it truly love?'

I weathered my mother's lashless eyes boring a slow, fine hole into my face. I nodded, staring all the while at the floor.

'Go,' said Trivediji, in a moment, 'and fetch me cold water from the next room.'

Briefly, I groped for a pitcher in an unlit space as he said to my dispirited mother: 'Cast out your fear, mataji. Your daughter is pure, pure as the Ganga that flows through the Himalayas.' He meant I was a virgin.

Ratna winced. 'It's Megha's marriage her father and I worry about. You see, this man's wife has some . . . letters of Megha's in her possession . . .'

Trivediji rocked with laughter. 'Love letters, hehn? And she intends to use them . . . most unscrupulous woman, ho-ho-ho. Whenever you try to arrange a marriage for the maiden, there she will be with her folder . . . telling her favourite story. But never fear, your daughter here has beauty and learning. Above all, she is high-born, a kulina. The husband who is to come will bear her off by force, like Prithviraj . . . but, before that, we have to destroy the evil one's designs, don't we? Something must be done . . . Get me a coconut, Bansi.' An acolyte emerged from the shadows. 'Now put your hand here, Megha Lahiri, Sandilya gotra, and recite after me . . .' A mantra, the sprinkling of holy water, an amulet for my throat, and my mother opening her purse.

*

One afternoon, Ratna and I went for lunch with Suren, my father's younger brother, the army surgeon. Through my growing-up years I had looked upon him more as an irresponsible older sibling whose opinion was normally suspect. He had returned recently from a prisoner-of-war camp in Pakistan and now drank to excess. He was also unquenchably honest at all times. As we started on the fish, Suren said:

'Do you know Monica, Nilu's wife? Whenever we meet, the lady says: Your niece has a boyfriend, and guess who it is ... my very own darling husband. Is this true, Megha?' I didn't reply, for news had clearly travelled. Again and again, in different ways, Suren quizzed, Suren pronounced: 'You shouldn't have put your parents through this, you know.'

I felt the eyes of my mother and Suren's wife drill into me, wanting a rise, an admission, public remorse? I wanted to scream. Frigidly, I turned to Suren. 'That's something between my parents and me, don't you think? In any case, it's my life. I'll live it like I want to.' He nodded, and I felt sorry to have snubbed this harmless busybody ... yet at that moment, it seemed the only way to bring to a halt the public unclothing to which I was now ceaselessly subjected, the tyranny of my mother's sad, denuding eyes.

Afterwards, as I washed my hands at the sink, Suren – who would not let it go – came up from behind to say bluntly, kindly: 'It's the love you didn't get as a child from your parents, Megha, that's what you're really after. Don't think you can get it from others, my girl, it just isn't around.'

I wanted to hug and to hit him at once for his cold perspicacity, his shattering a last illusion. So he too had seen what I'd felt only subliminally all those years, a mortal chill come to sit in the bone, an emptiness and my mother's hopeless shrinking ... Ratna, who heard the remark, withdrew quietly.

In Benares, I resumed my evening walks on the terrace, up and down, up and down, till the moon came up and the conch downstairs was blown. Biren, I am told, believed that I was pining for Nilu, but the truth is I hardly thought about him at all. I had instead these witty, reflective conversations with the interesting men and women I would meet one day, imagining how they would clamour for my friendship. Once, I overheard my father say with quiet emotion: 'My daughter is a small, soft bud, a pearl ... The things that woman said to her!' I just walked and walked, and made plans of future grandeur.

CHAPTER TWENTY

Beni Madho awoke with a start from a mid-morning nap, his school in summer recess. The animal next door had turned up his radio, relaying lunatic songs in Bhojpuri about a pinjere-wali-muniya, some damned depraved bird in a cage, a parrot ... Swallowing his rage and pride, he had been to see Ujala one last time at the house in Civil Lines. The Gurkha asked him to wait and swaggered indoors, emerging quickly afterwards to announce that Ujala-bi was not at home. As he spoke, Beni Madho heard the voices of women and stifled explosions from a half-crazed peasant, her unmistakable laugh. 'Told you, haven't I?' said the doorman, touching Beni Madho insultingly on the shoulder. 'She's gone out.'

He now stayed home all day, sullen, confined to the bedroom. He'd even lost some weight. It was two months since Ujala had left him, but neither food nor his friends' irreverent chatter had the power yet to coax him out of his misery. Between women, one can only suppose, thought Damyanti uncharitably, making no allowances for his age, his diminishing resilience. The dancing girl, God give him shame, had thrown him out at last from her palace of distorting mirrors.

He awoke that morning from a dream about the time –

just after Holi – when he had first married Damyanti. The young bride serving him his meals gravely in the kitchen, opalescent and arresting as the moon. He remembered her bangles of green and gold glass, clinking and clinking on the night he had first made her body his own. Between chores, doing the beds or dishes, he had heard her deep-throated song sometimes, but it disturbed him. It spoke of depths, maybe longings, in his wife that had no relation to him or his life with her, and which Beni Madho could not bear. He found fault at such times with her choice of music, hinting that music could be had even in a courtesan's house. Damyanti had sulked after these conversations, but he had always praised her beauty the same night with his hard, sweating body or made recompense with an attentive, teasing love. Who am I, said Damyanti to herself as the habit of singing began to fade, hardly Rasoolan Bai. I've a household to care for now, and a good husband.

When his mother had died and Beni Madho had fallen into debt, Damyanti had come to him one evening, placing two gold bangles on his upturned palm. 'Take these,' she said, 'they aren't any use to me. I feel in my bones,' she added, after a pause, 'that with Ammaji gone, you will slowly drift away, become a stranger to this house.' She could be so absurd. Beni Madho had taken her by the wrist and led her to their creaky bed with a sharp and uncontrollable desire. Soon afterwards, he had gone for an inoculation against cholera and met a hospital nurse who – having buried a whiny, critical husband a year ago – was preparing now to reveal high spirits to somebody of discernment. Beni Madho, it turned out, was just such a man.

In a storeroom leading off from the kitchen, with its tins of unground spice and pickle jars, stood Damyanti, turning the leaves of a yellowing book that listed the characteristics of a score of Indian ragas. The trouble with having Beni Madho home for the summer was that her singing had had to stop . . . She leaned her back on a shelf, humming over and over a favourite bandish in bhairavi that gave her life the lie. Laaga chunri mein daag, I have a stain on my veil that will not wash away. Is it any use, said Damyanti to herself, feeling suddenly desperate. She had applied to three schools for the post of music teacher and been turned away each time. Am I to scrub pots and nag the grime off collars for the rest of my life, waiting for Beni Madho? So he may eat, throw things and growl at me . . . to let me know that I exist after all. And each time he goes off to a new woman, I shall wring my sari's damp edge and run after him, hoping to stanch his urgency a little, his awful need.

They had asked at the schools for a degree called B. Mus. I've done music for high school and the inter-mediate, she had said, and I sing better than all my teachers.

'But you haven't a degree,' they had wailed. 'How will you teach musical theory?'

At one place, they agreed that what children really needed was someone to interest them first in classical music, teaching the movement of a raga almost in play, through songs and little exercises. The rest would come by practice and exposure. (Listening to you, said Ashwin Krishna once, I feel even I could learn to sing. It seems like so much fun.) Who were these kindly, dusty school administrators to judge the proficiency of a musical adept? They had little music themselves, they freely admitted. Hence the need for a degree . . . Damyanti saw herself knitting woollens for children in future years, embroidering little frocks and selling them to a shop in Katra. Which instantly brought on the tears for she cared nothing about clothes, and children's dresses, even less.

Ashwin entered just as Damyanti was quitting the storeroom, loosening her hair from its tight, oiled plait. She had cut it off up to the waist when Beni Madho had had his first affair, the hospital nurse. It wasn't defiance, just a loss in the energy it took to groom knee-length hair every day. Beni Madho had been furious. Turning into a memsahib, he had said, to show whom, if I may ask. He heard Ashwin's voice speaking to Damyanti in the kitchen now. The lodger had returned from vacation last night, and the morning was agog with his adventures in some ghostly, moonless place in the Almora hills. What could a learned fellow like him have to say to his silent, grey wife, wondered Beni Madho. It went on, and in a while, he heard Damyanti recount with muted laughter an incident with a policeman in the colony that Beni Madho knew nothing of. He could stand it no longer.

'Dammo,' he called, emerging from the bedroom, 'where are my clean things? Don't stand chattering like a parrot all morning, I have to have my bath.' He'd called her Dammo, as he used to in the first few years of marriage. She handed him a dhoti, a white vest and a thin cotton towel, looking briefly into his face. Damyanti then walked back to the kitchen, wordless as an effigy and as unblinking.

She had little humour for her own husband, thought Beni Madho, you had to say that. Beneath her staring and slow walk, perhaps she didn't feel much, anyway, or think of things beyond the afternoon meal. Yet the lecturer from England talked to Damyanti for up to an hour sometimes . . . was it from a lack of female company? On the other hand, maybe she wasn't such a half-wit after all, just somebody who hadn't given Beni Madho's family an heir. A creature with the blood of his proud, clever race flowing through its little veins . . .

CHAPTER TWENTY-ONE

Six months later, I was back in Allahabad, to teach at the university in a leave vacancy. The professors who interviewed me saw that I had the marks, and the need to share (with minds as excitable as my own) some of the things that I had read or keenly felt. They also saw something wild in my eyes and felt that I needed the job. Perhaps I did, I cannot say, but it began again, a quietly satisfying life of reading and making notes for lectures through the night, of keeping a diary in which I told with numerous divagations and parentheses – and in so far as I could admit it at all – the truth about myself. I was a paying guest at the time with a very old lady who wanted only that her tenant should make no conversation. I did not return to 18 Church Lane, which had changed unrecognizably with Bela having married a bank officer and moved to Calcutta. Her husband was reported to be a coarse and pleasant man, who revealed over the years a large heart and a level of sexual activity that made Bela very happy indeed. Sreela, too, had left with her brood to join her husband, a taciturn civil engineer on a site in deepest Assam, and live in tents, drinking in the land-scape, pining for human contact ... As the story of my letters had reached Allahabad, I didn't dare to call upon

Mami. I also never found out whether she clammed her heart finally shut to Nilu, only that to the end of her days – punishing her for strong feelings and a sad ignorance, her tortured motherhood – the son never attempted to visit Mami again.

On weekends, a handful of us, teachers and men taking the IAS, would gather for tea in a broken-down house belonging to somebody's absent aunt. We said little on those afternoons that provoked any thought, just sat in the winter sun, letting each other be, free of expectation or fear, grateful to be alive. Occasionally the host, a grave young man with profound social concerns, would fix an exquisite punch with the fragrance of cloves, cinnamon and the more mysterious oriental herbs, and as the romantic chipped blue cup passed from hand to hand, one of us would read aloud the lines of Arvind Mehrotra, a local poet, to the invading dusk.

In this group or at the faculty common rooms some-times, I met Ashwin Krishna. The play we'd chosen had never come off, there'd been student strikes and the university had closed down for two months, but we were well acquainted by this time. On the mornings he came into the English staff room, he usually asked what I was teaching for the day. We talked about the poet and his period, Ashwin going quickly pedantic each time, armed to the teeth with social history, that is, on whatever we happened to discuss. He seemed interested, on the other hand, in everything and everybody around him.

'Can I tempt you to relax sometimes?' he once said, with his normal impudence. 'You're amazingly tense.'

I wasn't feeling any different from other mornings, no spasms or clutchings inside, so I said: 'I'm not tense, not particularly. Whatever gave you the idea?'

'Aren't you?' he gently asked, as though we were in a

film. 'Look at your fists, they're tightly clenched ... all the time. Makes me a little afraid of you.' He took my right hand in his, prizing it open with a long finger. There were nail marks in the palm. My nails, as it happened, were painted, a flashy, leaping scarlet, something fashionable. He turned my palm over and studied the varnish, frowning, addressing me with the familiar 'tu':

'Do your hands look better, stained this way?' If he has to ask, they obviously don't, I thought, but to him I said something rude, something that I prefer to forget.

Another time, we stood beneath a marquee, an assorted group of teachers with the bay of four moribund shehnais at our backs. The daughter of the head of English being wed ... I wore a smart, pale lipstick, maybe a little eye shadow, and was in the middle of greeting somebody when Ashwin showed up and placed a chaste finger on my lips. Parul, Vijay, Sanat, he called out to our friends, and taking me by the shoulders, twirled me once lightly round. 'Good people,' said he with an unfailing good humour, 'doesn't she look superbly artificial?' Protests and laughter from the friends. I should have taken offence, but he was so corny, so clearly a man without ego himself, it was hard to feel anything at all.

Next morning, in the common room, he handed me a paperback with a woman's torso impaled upon its cover, *The Female Eunuch*. I took it home, and read it slowly over a week. When the author asked women to taste their menstrual blood, I sat back, amused, here was a woman out to shock, to draw — in whatever manner she could — attention to herself. Menstrual blood, she explained, was the purest thing in creation. At more propitious times, it went to nourish a baby. By the end of the book, I wasn't feeling superior at all. Tragically, and without question, I was one of a tribe that didn't particularly like itself, its body or the body's functions, and felt good or real only when somebody out there told us that we were so. Why didn't women dare to leave their homes without 'necessary adornment' (lipstick, earrings, fashionable clothes)? Men seemed to manage well enough without these things ... A lot of the time, we spoke, did, even tried to feel, the things that others were willing us to. Didn't we think ourselves good enough the way we were? Momentarily, I had the mouth-watering vision of a woman in her home, quietly flaunting her body (a taut, pale flank and bare shoulders), of bragging about her talent with colours or dance, of gently silencing a man, you don't know, I'll tell you. Was it what I wanted for myself? Not quite. I did, however, want to declare (not through speech, but the way I lived): This is what I am, and how I wish to be loved, with my failure to confront people, warts, solitariness and all ... When I met Ashwin again, I found him wholly foreign still to the things that I understood, beauty and being finely differentiated, and living with intensity for a few things at a time. He was also the only emancipated man of my acquaintance, someone at once more deeply connected with people and more unapologetically free in a personal sense than I. His face had about it a certain ascetic quality, the eyes and mouth lustrated, made finer in my mind by tragic childhood events. When turned to me, they became merely severe.

One morning, as I was taking Keats with one of the rowdier undergraduate groups, I saw Ashwin slipping in behind a desk in the back row with its inkstains and graffiti, and pupils with everything except lessons on their mind. The rowdies beside him simmered, then grew quiet. He really had no business entering my class without asking, but just then we were doing the 'Ode on Melancholy':

> Or if thy mistress some rich anger shows,
> Emprison her soft hand and let her rave,
> And feed deep, deep upon her peerless eyes.

The students and I felt at once the dominion of a woman's low tone, the lover devouring in the same moment her softness and blue gaze. It was a relentless poet who could bear to leave no sense of his reader unstained or without a quiver. Afterwards, Ashwin Krishna and I drove out to Civil Lines in a second-hand motor car he had bought. For lunch at Kwality. Fish cutlets, vanilla ice cream and air conditioning that juddered and went out at least twice in the course of a warm afternoon.

'You were brilliant,' he nodded after we had ordered, choosing his words with care. 'I could feel an agitation in the young breasts. Yet, if you'll forgive me, I think you're no educator. Or are you?'

'You mean I can't teach?' I asked, pouncing hungrily on some creamy bread. Ready that moment to dismiss anything at all that he might have to say.

'Oh, you can,' he waved, silencing an unseen heckler. 'You teach well. It's that you don't simplify at all, you talk to about five people in the class and the rest can go home and take a nap for all you care. Why have you come to this drab profession? Not to give of yourself, surely. It's for some other reason . . . adulation, testing your ideas . . . to learn more yourself?'

When asked like that, I couldn't for the life of me say why. It was not that I liked an audience . . . all those eyes, yet after a while, once we had our teeth into the subject, it got entirely bearable. For the minds before me were young and excited by new things, and beneath the swagger, mainly unprejudiced. 'What are you suggesting?' I asked Ashwin. 'That I snub the curious and eager ones who've come to the text full of questions, and turn it into a class for grim note-takers? The ones for whom life itself is a big examination? With, mercifully, divisions and ranks and gold medals waiting at the end?'

'That's not who I'm talking about,' he interjected bluntly. 'A teacher must also mediate between the difficulty of an idea in its context and the innocence of the mind preparing to receive it ... I think you need to assume more ignorance in your listeners, to repeat yourself, to illustrate ... It *is* an alien sensibility you're describing, an idiosyncratic foreign tongue.'

'That's a bit grand,' I couldn't help saying, 'to assume nobody's heard of anything until they enter the portals of your class, or that when they leave, they'll have everything pat about a poet's work and time, his whole philosophy, just like that. My teachers never talked down to me. They made books exciting by ... by showing the connections with life and giving a name to my sensations. It was the particular, the fat grape or sharp-edged blade of grass, they taught me to roll first on my tongue.' Then I drove it in: 'By your lights, perhaps it's okay to sink a whole body of political opinion into a mind that is too callow yet to form its own? Perhaps it makes life easier for your pupils in some way?'

Ashwin grinned, his face colouring slightly. 'You're being an ass,' he said, very low. 'It's there already, the politics, in all we say or do. A sneaky little viper, if not taken firmly by the teeth. I just point it up, show people the corners of its lurking ... is that wrong? I talk politics in class because I don't like the soft, unhurt faces in the front rows, these fellows've got here straight from their mothers ... The world out of college isn't a fair place, full of luck or easy on the weak. I want these youngsters to go away less innocent, less quiescent before injustice. And opposed ... definitely opposed to inflicting it when their turn comes.'

Which didn't sound too much like the anticipated defence of a rabble rouser. Though maybe that's all he was, a man with political ambitions, waiting patiently to don the Gandhi cap one day, and kiss old women and children with running noses as they frowned at him in the blistering midday heat. Right then, squinting into a soup that tasted suspiciously like chicken curry, his thoughts seemed far away. His furrowed mouth looked incapable of kissing anybody, leave alone babies or the destitute. I decided to make an effort, talk about myself:

'Have you noticed how insistent you get about the things that are wrong with me? If I'm to believe you, I'm tense, I'm artificial, I'm even dishonest in my profession ... perhaps you've heard that I've recently been through a bad relationship. Can't one be let off getting one's act together perfectly, at least some of the time?'

Ashwin laughed, probably at my self-pity, the demand for special treatment. His eyes looked suddenly sharper through the glasses, puzzled, figuring something out. 'Yes,' he said, a trace of boredom in his voice, 'I've heard about the uncle, from Tara. In several episodes, blow by blow. Tara doesn't leave much out. Incidentally, she felt that you opened yourself out too much, too early, that was your fault. She also told it like a very romantic story.'

I thought of Monica, Nilu's wife, her giggling and sudden screams, her saying: 'Eat a rosogolla, Megha.'

Gently, my left temple began to throb, there were the letters in my looped, slanting hand, the guilty, nothing-denying letters.

'Shall I tell you something else?' continued Ashwin, as if anything short of a public flogging would stop him now. 'The reason you suffer is not because you squander yourself, far from it, but because you calculate. You hold back. Is he coming far enough forward, do I let him take my space?'

'Which is what you believe I did with the "uncle", right? Let me tell you, you haven't a clue.'

'About you or the way things work?' he asked, full once again of an indomitable good nature.

'Either. I don't think you listen to what people say at all. Did you understand anything beyond the pretty tale told by our disloyal Tara? That there can sometimes be circumstances beyond our control? I doubt it.' For there it was again, Professor Krishna on his hobby-horse, Megha's Many Faults. He will give you, on the one hand, *The Female Eunuch* to read and, with the other, steadily whittle away at your separateness, your control ... 'What, according to you,' I asked, smiling but angry, 'is the decent thing to be? A profligate with one's favours, all things to all men?'

He was laughing again. 'Jesus, no,' he said, ending with a sigh. 'Look, we're all of us distinct (and alone) without even trying to be. And if life has her way, that's how we shall probably remain, it's the human condition. Yet in order to connect with others, students, parents, somebody of the opposite sex, we have to decide at some point to break down the walls of our personal cages, don't you think, let it all hang out? It seems absurd to notch up one's gains in a relationship, to say if he gives so much, I'll give some ... The idea is to let go, little lady, to merge, to give another human being the seat by the fire. And maybe some of the warmth will come back to you.'

Merge, emerge, I scarcely knew what he spoke of. (Had the man ever known what it was like to get your nose slowly rubbed in the dirt?) Yet if I just half-listened to Ashwin Krishna, an eavesdropper to somebody else's conversation, I knew I would understand exactly what.

'You're the romantic heroine,' he pronounced, with the triumph of calling something by its rightful name, 'who got everything right except loving. You put a fellow on his guard, a routine of unending good behaviour. What can he do except run away in the end?'

What a fool I'd been, it suddenly struck me, to let the conversation get personal, and allow this thoughtless, bounding bear to calmly rip open and eviscerate my defining traumas with a series of stinging, half-baked explanations. 'And you,' I said, keeping my voice calm, curious now about the limits of his conceit, 'you know how to do these things? Get the measure of giving just right in your relationships?'

Ashwin was silent. 'No,' he said at last, taking a stab at the impossible. Humility. 'There's little I do know that I can use in my own life. I believe in people, though, and keep trying to be better friends with the ones I've met. The thing is, I'm not afraid of looking ridiculous, so I'm usually the one to put my hand out first.' He frowned at the vanilla ice melting uncontrollably across his quarter-plate.

I wasn't going to show him I was angry. Or hurt. I wasn't going to do any of those things. If he wanted an argument, with accusations and the reddening of eyes to round off the afternoon, he wasn't going to get it. 'That was a lovely lunch,' I said with a cute tea-party expression. 'Thanks a lot.' It didn't hurt to smile at a fellow you were never going to see again. Who did he think he was? I wanted the afternoon to end quickly.

'Let's do this again,' said Ashwin to my surprise. You had to hand it to him, for stupidity. He was peering into my face now and looked displeased with what he saw. Arrogance, ahankar, the lady will not stoop to quarrel. Or defend herself. He wanted no truck with pride. There were, mercifully, other things in the world, history, travel, even the honey-haired Susan, who wanted only that he live in England.

We waved with slack wrists as Ashwin dropped me off . . . It had begun and ended with my fast-growing list of shortcomings, and somebody's clever remedy for each. Nothing an afternoon nap would not cure. Or pitch into a deserved oblivion.

CHAPTER TWENTY-TWO

When Beni Madho saw Abdul Rafiq, the tailor, shuffling his feet outside the Government High School, gargling apologetically in the way he had with betel juice in his mouth, he knew that his friend had news for him. The seth's son, it turned out, was torturing his bulbul, Ujala. Not only was she immured with another mistress in a decaying house, but he beat her mercilessly if she danced or so much as spoke to an outsider. A woman from Katra, who had seen her briefly in an outsize motor car, reported a purple swelling over Ujala's eye, the contusions growing with every telling. It occurred to Beni Madho to gather up his friends, a bottle of something potent for himself, and attempt a rescue, but Ujala, he knew, would spit and call him names before everybody if he showed up at her door. Served the bitch right, he thought, entering his own front door, for grovelling to the young pervert, the diamond-peddler. The rich have no feeling, what did she expect. In a way, it was right, nature's law, that every woman should finally meet the man who would subdue her, tell her her place in the scheme of things. As he, Beni Madho, the shrewd and handsome Brahmin, had shown his wife, Damyanti, who when she came as a bride had

had a certain vanity, an unyieldingness, a tendency to sulk.

It was nearing two in the afternoon. She would be standing in the bedroom, watching him take off his shoes and wipe the cracked soles of his tired feet on the worn doormat. Or she might walk in from the kitchen with a look of guilt (on a day she had been to the market) to hand him clean clothes, letters, room rent from the lodger. Damyanti, in fact, was nowhere to be seen. He peeled off his damp kurta, hanging the sacred thread over his left ear as he hunted angrily for a dhoti and towel. Where in God's name was she? Woman, are you asleep or dead somewhere, he said aloud. The only reply was a series of rhythmical thuds from a grindstone in Urmila's courtyard ... Then he saw his clothes piled neatly on a chair in the wind-filled verandah.

After his wash, as Beni Madho dressed, he saw his wife bustle in through the front door, glistening and out of breath.

'Where have *you* been?' he asked, distaste curling his upper lip. She was forcing upon him a role he did not like, an interruption of the luxurious silence of years.

'At the neighbour's,' she replied, sucking an untimely clove. 'I wanted change for a tenner.'

You chose a very good time, thought Beni Madho sardonically, till something clicked in his sullen brain and he saw that she was dressed to go out. Starched cotton sari, her hair in a small, oiled bun, and a jhola with its few careful contents slung over her left shoulder. In her hand, she held a small string purse that carried her keys, small change and some cloves.

'Looks as if you're going somewhere,' he observed, using the formal 'you' reserved for sarcasm and outsiders. Damyanti muttered something about 'work' and 'being

194

late'. 'What was that?' snapped Beni Madho. 'Of course you're late. What work can you have at this hour?'

Here it was then, the moment she had fled from all her life, of truth, and all the anger and ugliness that went with it. Reluctantly, trembling a little, she straightened her back and looked Beni Madho full in the eyes. 'I haven't mentioned it earlier, but I've got myself a job.'

He chortled at first, ridicule sometimes being the quickest medicine. 'Doing what, if I may ask? What will anybody pay *you* money for . . . To wash dishes and mop the floor for some rich woman, who's too idle to get up off her own buttock?'

'No,' she calmly replied. 'I'll be teaching music to children at the Prayag Sangeet Samiti. For six hundred rupees a month.' It sounded to her like a small fortune. It was also the only place where, when she went, they had first asked her to sing. When Damyanti confessed that she had no degree, they had conferred amongst themselves, and announced that they needed to think it over. At a second interview, they made her teach a small class. Damyanti had shut her eyes and conjured from memory all the ruses (coaxing, games and charm) by which, many years ago, she'd got her sisters to sing. A hymn to Saraswati in bhairavi. The talented class at the Prayag had picked up the song – with its luring flats and quick beat – joyfully, in a ripple . . . Left to herself, Damyanti would never have tried the famous music school, it needed a terrible audacity, but the lodger upstairs nagged till she went. After her second interview, Ashwin had met the Vice Chancellor, asking him to put in a word, but when the slow elder with his beetling white brows finally called the school, Damyanti Misra had already been hired.

Beni Madho was beside himself. The nerve, the pure flaming cheek of the woman. As if he could have his wife going about town, flaunting her accomplishment and big breasts, turning him into the laughing stock. Wouldn't the men say Misra was living off his wife's earnings?

'Woman,' he said in a voice that first rose, then cracked with frustration, the unreasonableness of it all, 'have you taken leave of your senses? Don't I bring home enough to fill your large belly? Get these cheap and foolish notions out of your head, you're going nowhere. And first, get rid of that miserable widow's dress.'

Damyanti did not budge.

Beni Madho went so red in the face, you thought he would burst a blood vessel. 'I won't stand for it,' he shouted. 'My wife going out and earning her keep just the same as a common slut. What is it you want, that men should peer into your sari and stand there licking their lips every morning? Put one foot out of that door and I'll . . .' Suddenly, he lunged forward and, with his left hand, snatched Damyanti's purse from her.

She shrieked, reaching out to retrieve it, but Beni Madho laughed unpleasantly and moved away, holding the purse up, out of her reach. 'Give it back,' wailed Damyanti. 'Give me my batua, you've no right . . .'

'And if I don't, what are you going to do?' said her husband, his eyes flashing.

'You can't keep my purse, you have to . . .' Damyanti tried to grab his arm, but he turned, and moved still further away. 'You brute, you good-for-nothing, where do you think you'll go with my few paise, anyway?'

Beni Madho looked at her in surprise, the woman was beginning to get offensive.

'You've taken everything, my speech, my laughter, my singing,' she continued. 'You've locked me up and turned me into an animal.' It seemed to be vanishing with the bead purse, her last chance of putting the bits of her life together, of becoming human again. Damyanti was scream-ing now: 'You always told me I was a freak. I know who the freak is now, it's you that destroys everything he touches, you're a raakshas. And now, you've come for the last drop of life I have left in me. I hate your leer, the touch of your hand. Give me that purse.'

Beni Madho was looking at his wife with his mouth open, she was like a woman possessed. Something must have happened to loosen so many words from Damyanti, he couldn't believe the woman had them in her. 'That's enough,' he said uncertainly. She looked like she might pick up something any moment, an umbrella, a pan, and take it to her husband. Then the neighbours would come in, and where would his izzat be.

'I curse you,' screeched Damyanti. 'I curse your rela-tives, and I curse the day that I set foot in this house.'

Then, as suddenly, she became silent, beads of sweat starting up on her forehead and upper lip. Her face was flushed, she still wanted to shout I spit on you, and, if she could, knock two of his front teeth out. It kept spilling out of her brain, one poisoned thought after another, murderous, molten, and reckless of consequence. Then the tears started up, of bitterness and failure, except she wouldn't let them flow. I've botched it, she thought, this is not how I wanted to do things. I meant to go out of that door quickly, before he came in, without expla-nations. And the boy upstairs, he's going to say the same thing. You've done it all wrong, he'll say.

Beni Madho was now sitting on a takhat, waiting to see what his wife would do next, this rasping, snarling tigress with claws. He had forgotten how tall she was, how straight she had begun to hold herself lately. Damyanti watched him with exasperation.

'If you had any shame or reason,' she said, taking the

purse from his slack fingers, 'I would have tried to talk. But look at you . . . a cheek not shaven for a week, a body that heaves, pants and is robbed of its pride, a character all eaten with greed. For the silliest of things, a string of spoilt women.' Somebody called out Damyanti's name, it was Urmila, saying a rickshaw had arrived and was waiting at the door. 'I'll be plain with you,' said Damyanti, 'what I do from now on is my business. Nothing obliges me to discuss my plans any more . . . I feel completely free of you. And if teaching children brings shame upon this house, you can start with quitting your job first. I'm late today . . . Some other time, if you really want to understand what has happened, I'll try and explain.'

Beni Madho sat like a distraught, wild-eyed water balloon, watching its leaked entrails upon the ground. Where was the woman he had subdued, who knew him incontrovertibly as master? This was kaliyuga, the age of evil, in its fullness. 'Somebody's put you up to this,' he blubbered. 'Going against your own husband. If you leave now, who will give me my lunch? Somebody's got to be home in the afternoons, we can't all be out.'

'That's right, we can't,' snapped Damyanti, eyes like marbles. 'Your lunch is waiting for you in the kitchen. Give yourself what you want, then, in two thalis, serve out portions for the boy and for me. We'll eat when we get back. As for somebody being here, I think you said that you've finished work for the day? It's up to you now to guard the old ruin I've haunted for twenty-five years. Who knows, you may even get to like it.'

He took a step towards her, threatening with the short, thick half-swipe of the corpulent, part of a long role. 'Don't be a fool,' said Damyanti softly. 'People laugh at you for being jilted by a whore. Don't make them split their sides, saying his old wife flew the coop, too, serves the old miser right.' Beni Madho fell back, stung.

The rickshaw-wallah was ringing his bell continuously, in a single long trill now. It's a hot sun, mataji, have pity on me. Urmila stood at the gate to see Damyanti off for her first day at work. 'I'll meet you in the evening,' said her flustered neighbour, settling herself a little awkwardly on the rickshaw. Urmila's pregnant daughter stood in the doorway, rubbing her eyes, exchanging a look of relief and complicity with her mother. And a small germ of hope ... for their daughters, granddaughters, women in the neighbourhood? Meanwhile, the twin soporifics of domesticity and a day temperature of forty degrees centigrade would take their toll. They went slowly indoors.

CHAPTER TWENTY-THREE

For a long time, he stood at the end of the platform, far from the vendors, coolies and the bookstall, staring down at the railtrack. There wouldn't be a train for hours yet. As he had entered the station, Ashwin had felt that he suddenly understood why the students of the city came here every day: life was a mess, but when you saw the frenzied movement of people, the trains coming and then going away, felt coal in your nostrils and shouting in your ears, you knew that it would all of it, good or bad, pass. And you'd be left with activity and laughter, perhaps a more good-humoured acceptance of the fact that when things worked, they were never in the ways you wanted them to.

Ashwin had recently been offered a teaching fellowship at Magdalen, his old college at Oxford, but when he came down to tell his landlady this evening, she had described in disturbing detail her exchange with Beni Madho on her first day of work. Ashwin had looked at her with the same expression as Beni Madho, shocked, with his mouth open: 'But those weren't the things to say, you've done it all wrong,' he muttered in alarm.

The woman began to cry, a film of wetness gaining on her cheek. From frustration at her own weakness, the things she'd said. Yet how would a man, a mere youth, know the anger she felt, a frantic, throttling beast that strained inside, threatening to rip and maul everything in sight? 'You haven't been married to Beni Madho for twenty-five years,' was all she managed to say.

'No,' he nodded, tugging at his moustache, watching her as she blew her nose. Have I loosed something in this woman that will destroy her in the end? We do not know our power. 'You have to live with him many years,' he had said to Damyanti. 'Some day you'll have to tell him what you need ... there's no way out. If he doesn't like what you do, he'll learn to live with it, anyway. Poor Misraji, ever since that Ujala business, he's begun to walk like an old man, tired, shuffling his feet, as if each of them weighed a ton.'

With a growing despondency, he thought of Megha, the dark-eyed girl with her impassioned movements of neck and shoulders in conversation. She was both comical and touching in her intensity, but without a trace of humour in her little body. She took things hard, her circumstances, her feelings, all that others said to her. It was the way she'd taken him, seriously, weighing his every word, and she wasn't going to forgive anything. I seem to have run into the darkest alley of this city, blind inside sunglasses, thought Ashwin, and trampled one by one all the smaller, softer animals underfoot ... Damyanti, Megha. And I will never learn. It's best I clear out and go to England now, to the punts and long waving grass beside the river, lager and pale skies. Who knows, I may even meet Susan again. He hadn't, in fact, thought of Susan for weeks, her laughter or the fine gold of her hair. Or her questions, for Susan Knightley was always asking questions. Why can't you have a drink with your father? What did he send you to boarding school for? What, why? It was fun talking to her, sometimes even making up explanations that she would understand, but you couldn't spend your life trying to put the entire boring past into words. A walking memoir . . . It was nice for a change to be taken at face value, as if the present counted for something. One afternoon, he had walked with Megha in the rain, under the broad-leafed mango trees of Poonappa road. They had been silent for a while, shivering slightly, letting the warm rain soak into their skins. Then Ashwin suddenly skidded on some moss, and lay flat on his back under a tree. Megha, who had watched him round-eyed, walked up to where he lay, and then next minute, she too slipped on the rich, wet mud. They had sat there, splattered, laughing like luna-tics, as rows of cyclists passed, silent and curious, on their way home from work, the rain gently sibilant on their tyres . . . That was a girl with whom, when she talked, you had this uncontrollable urge to touch her mouth with your fingertips. Like Damyanti, she had a fund of anger inside her but, unlike the older woman, a repelling pride and a certain lack of charity. He was lucky to be leaving.

As he brooded, a youth in a tight cap and blue-and-yellow patterned shirt had walked up to him unnoticed. Ashwin raised his head, recognizing the student who had angrily spurned his interest the first time they met at Prayag. What right had he, the boy had demanded, to offer silken hope to a generation whose future in terms of jobs was a deep black pit? Does he want another argument, thought Ashwin glumly. He's chosen the wrong day . . . I'm tired and, in the important things, I can see that I have failed. Maybe I'll tell him that. They greeted each other, and fell silent again.

'I hear that you're leaving Allahabad,' said the youth at last. 'Is it for good?'

Ashwin stared. How did the fellow know, he hadn't mentioned it to anybody yet. Or maybe just to the head of his department. 'I can't say,' he replied, hesitating, 'but then none of my plans are for good. How's it going with you? Studying madly for the exams?'

The youth removed his cap, revealing a shaven skull that transformed him at once into a schoolboy, pubertal and somehow at the mercy of his onlookers. 'My father died two weeks ago. From now on, I have to support my mother and sisters. I won't be able to continue my studies, I'm afraid.'

'I'm sorry,' said Ashwin with caution. 'What are you planning to do?'

'Actually, it was my father who wanted me to go to college, I'm not much good with books or writing things out. My chacha, who owns a printing press but has no sons of his own, has asked me to help out.'

'But it is what you want?' asked Ashwin, openly curious now.

'In a way, yes,' replied the youth. Name of Verma, Ramkumar Verma. 'I can't wait to start on "real life", money in your hands, getting married, seeing other cities ... I've had enough of books and imagining what it's like out there. I know that it won't be easy.'

They were silent for a while, thinking their separate thoughts till Ashwin looked up again, to see Ramkumar wiping his eyes. 'For the past five years,' he said, 'I have shown my father nothing but contempt, a hatred even. He was a miser, I told him, a failure and a bore. I said it from the fear that I would grow up to be like him, and never amount to anything ... The only material object that man was ever attached to was a radiogram he'd bought himself some years ago, he liked music. I sold it off last year to give myself a holiday in the hills . . . I miss Babuji. To the end, I think, he still loved me.'

For a long time, the two stood staring down at a torn red rag, an ebullient weed, dried faeces and the shining metal of the track below. The light had begun to dim. As they walked out of the platform, Ashwin saw a tea-seller raise his hand in a salute and thought of his friend, Udai Bir Singh. Udai had not been seen for over a month. He turned to Verma:

'Have you any news of Dr Singh? I hear he's gone out of town.'

Ramkumar looked at him in surprise. 'Haven't you heard, Dr Singh is in Bombay, that's the place where his wife comes from. There's some trouble between them, we hear he's filed for a divorce.' Ashwin shook the youth's hand, trying to conceal his amazement, then held him once, lightly, by the shoulder.

'What I've learnt,' said the innocent Ramkumar, 'is that time in this place is uncertain. Who knows which of us will be missing tomorrow. There's one thing we must fight to keep, our bond with each other. We can't let people walk out.'

Tonight, thought Ashwin, as he bicycled slowly past the university, he would explain to Damyanti that she would have to talk to Beni Madho. Next week, next month . . . for dialogue was the key, the source of power. It was also the only way to find peace, with oneself even. He thought of Ramkumar's words as he passed the English department; we mustn't break our links with others, it's all we've got, we can't let people go, and began pedalling faster, faster. At the turning for Beni Madho's house, he almost collided with a rickshaw and stopped, his mind as clear as the September sky in Allahabad, and as firm in its purpose. There were plenty of things that could still go wrong, but by tomorrow he would have a detailed plan, an irrevocable course of action. Which he would flog, if necessary, till he dropped dead on the ground.

CHAPTER TWENTY-FOUR

It was nearly two months since that lunch at Kwality, where Ashwin Krishna and I had wasted no time in exposing (with a wealth of pithy phrases) each other's pitiful affectations and weakness. Nor had we met since, except in large groups, which was all to the good as both knew now how hollow they were, our attempts at talk and personal exploration, even good fellowship. A complete waste with some, leaving behind only a small, bitter, parched feeling that both of us could do without. And since there were no direct trains from Allahabad yet, by a route of flat brown fields that led halfway round the subcontinent I was on my way now to Bombay. To attend a drama workshop organized by Prithvi Theatres, along with Vishal Joshi, Reader in Hindi, who was said to have written two plays in Bhojpuri. He was somebody I had never seen before.

The train had left Allahabad twenty minutes ago and there was no evidence of Vishal Joshi yet. It had me slightly worried. Already the grim, middle-aged couple on the facing berth, who had examined with a speechless censure every unappeasing detail of my appearance and skimpy luggage, had begun to unpack a mouth-watering meal of poories, fried potato and mango pickle. The man looked up as if he would ask me to join them, but was silenced in time by a steely look in his thin wife's eyes ... Suddenly, it felt wonderful to be getting away from my schedule of anxious swotting and pretending to know all the answers before a packed class of large innocents. It was not that I minded revealing my ignorance or powerlessness, my lack of words, just that — as the youngest member of the faculty — it felt like I had to prove something. That I was serious about my profession? That I actually had something to give to people younger than I was? For a while now, it would be Chowpatty and the sea, meeting playwrights and actors (maybe even Shashi Kapoor), and chats with other theatre buffs in a smokefilled coffee house ... Outside my window was the dark night, with the trees, dwellings and bushes we swept past mere shapes of possibility, giving place now and then to clusters of timid reddish-yellow lantern light whenever we passed a village. The conductor had just entered and sat himself on my berth in a dusty navy blue to check our tickets, when a young man in grey trousers, silk shirt and tie loomed suddenly in the narrow door, a jacket slung over his shoulder. My, I thought, aren't we grand tonight! It was Ashwin, plague and world-changer, looking as if he was in a play, causing me sudden and inexplicable regret for being dressed in a dark brown khadi kurta.

'What are you doing here?' I said.

He let himself in. 'Going to Bombay, same as you, for the Prithvi theatre workshop. Actually, Joshi was chosen, he has all sorts of ideas on theatrical technique, but he could take it or leave it, he said, so I came along instead.'

'I didn't know you were so keen on theatre,' I said, cranky, resenting him. He would be a terrible companion for the trip, critical, cocksure, a Mr Know-all. There, I thought, goes my sweet break from everyday life.

'I didn't either,' he replied, grinning, his hair too long. 'Who knows what further inclinations I may reveal before the trip is over?'

'Except this train goes to Delhi,' I drily observed, groaning inside of me. Some people never changed. Nor had his name been anywhere on the list pasted outside the carriage door.

'So it does,' said Ashwin Krishna, 'but from where we live, isn't this still the shortest route to Bombay?' Neither of us knew. It was also a longish conversation to have had over the conductor's peaked cap, as he fidgeted to rise and leave our cramped quarters.

'I want a nap before dinner,' I finally announced. Best to tackle it moment by moment, I thought, contend with aggravation in small ways. 'We got to bed last night at three.' There had been a small party with some girls writing Ph.D.s in physics, cigarettes behind closed doors and stories of other people's marriages.

'Right,' said Ashwin, vanishing as suddenly as he had materialized.

Around ten fifteen, the silent grey-haired couple in my compartment (the droop of disapproval now branded permanently down the sides of their mouths) were preparing for bed. They unfolded with a fierce concentration a case full of clothes, sheets, pillowcases in tasteless checks and a shaded embroidery as if they had all week on the train, and would never have to get off.

He put his head in through the door. 'We never really talked about Germaine Greer. Do you agree with her description of female sexuality?' he asked loudly of a sweetly humming train.

The couple looked as if they had discovered a small bomb in the carriage. Their suspicions about my appearance were confirmed: the lesser the adornment and anxiety to be liked, the greater the likely depravity of the brain. 'It feels a bit stuffy in here,' I quickly said. 'Couldn't we stand by the main door a few minutes?' I felt wide awake as we walked down the corridor.

The train stopped then with a gnash, a long squeak and a low juddering, far away from any place. It waited almost thirty minutes, a stubborn, crouching animal in the dark. We spoke of the pavement bookstores of Bombay, Germaine Greer and our friends in the English department. It was almost amiable. Then he fell silent for what seemed like ten minutes and stood looking out at the trees. I thought of going back to the cabin, retiring for the night, when he said:

'You met my friend Udai Singh, didn't you? Well, he had this boy in his class who dressed like Rajesh Khanna, the little toff, and gave himself all the airs of a city man. Apparently his father came to see him, a plain peasant in a dhoti, turban and earrings, who even carried his shoes in his hand. As he was leaving, the man overheard his son declare to his mates in the next room: That's no relative of mine, yaar, just an ignorant peasant who works for my father. At a little distance from his village, Udai told me, the old gent hung himself from a tree. This was the son he had worked like a beast all his life to raise and educate ... Udai and I asked ourselves: If these are the monsters we turn out, there has to be something grievously wrong with our teaching, with university education in this country.' He became silent again. For me at that moment, before the sweat and tears on an old man's lined, brown face as he trudged home in the heat, rejected by his worthless son, poetry, image and the discussion of sensibility began to seem terrifyingly useless. Yet if something more than a sense of the beautiful was needed to put us in touch with life, what was it? I watched Ashwin struggle with something as he looked out still, for once at a loss for words.

At last it came along, a huge slow hot engine on whose grunting passage our own depended, vomiting whole skies of black that covered and entered us, that dimmed our thoughts. It had barely passed when, without warning, our train took a long lurch. I was in the doorway, lightly clasping a steel bar, when I slipped. Inept thing to do, but as I lost the handle, my body met up instantly with blackness and very fresh, fast-moving air . . . only Ashwin was as quick. He got hold of a wrist somehow and yanked as hard as he could, lifting me right off the floor as I came in again.

I stood against a wall afterwards, facing the moss-green lavatory doors. We were breathing hard.

When he moved back, pinning me lightly to the wall with his fingers, Ashwin's eyes were wide, astonished. 'No, you don't,' he slowly said. 'Not till I've got my piece said.'

'Your piece,' I repeated, still in shock. 'Of course, the trouble with me . . . the things I don't do right.' At that moment, to be truthful, these were parrot words from the top of my head, to disguise as well as I might the cowardly, uncontrollable thumping of my heart. Outside the door, it had been very cold, my head somewhere near the carriage steps.

'That's the bit I've said already,' he shot back, sharp as a catapult. 'You haven't heard the rest. The reason I'm on this train tonight is to tell you I was wrong. In most of what I said, and certainly in *why* I said it.'

'No, you weren't,' I was forced to concede, bewildered now, for events were taking unforeseen twists one after the other, turning beasts to beauties, and his face so close. Danger mingled with the smell of phenyl and a coal dust that cut through everything, entering our hair and ears and skin. 'Some of your wretched speeches made sense. I got angry because most times you made it hard for me to like myself.'

He eyed me curiously, did people really have such brittle self-esteem? 'I was a pig, wasn't I,' he said, 'taking your actions apart, ladling out these ready-made personae you were expected to conform to ... The trouble is I took you to be more like me, which you aren't. Your impulses are ... emotional, poetic maybe, whereas mine are social and in search of defining theory. If you and I sometimes arrive at the same point in understanding events about us, it's usually by very different paths ... Yours direct, reaching the nerve, and mine ... mine perhaps more tolerant, more inclusive? There I go again ... but you see, my reason for picking holes all the time didn't lie with you at all. It was something in me, a disturbing need that I refused to acknowledge. And I came to grips with it in silly, cruel ways.'

It was clear by now that there were several kinds of danger – watching, stirring, waiting to pounce – if one stood too long at the door, so for a second time I prepared to retreat to my cabin. Which was when his mouth first touched mine briefly, and left. Light as the breast of an unfledged bird, a dragonfly's invisible wing. I tried to talk but his lips were on mine again, full, pressing with a first fugitive claim, a question ... it was very nice. I gave up worrying about coal dust and opened my mouth to let his moistness break in.

It was because of this absurd, provoking man that I'd encountered Germaine Greer and learned to like my body's rhythms and hair, my feet of clay. He kissed my nose and I knew that, with him, I would never pretend to being somebody I was not. Cool or cute or quiescent. His finger found a scar on my chin. If I reached for an idea, he would be there with it first, rapid as the tide, and as teasing. There would be no playing woman to an endangered male.

There came to mind letters I'd written (in a dead, unreal past) and a very real woman's voice, its harsh unfeeling tones, curdling the meaning of my sentences to obscenity, to dross.

'Have you a wife?' I asked, my voice going flat.

Ashwin looked at me as if I was crazy. I was, more than a little. That moment I also liked him more than I can say.

'I haven't,' he said very slowly, 'but I intend to before long. If she will have me, that is.'

Despite all courtesies to which I had been trained, all habits of denial, my back stiffened. I was a trapped hare. So there was somebody after all, tucked away in England or Benares, and there he stood, smiling at me in an ill-lit space before the lavatories. Weakly, I tried to disengage, but he caught me so tightly against him then, it hurt my breasts.

'Don't,' I said. 'It hurts.'

He loosened his grip, slightly. 'Ask me who it is,' he said, taking my hair in his mouth. 'I want you to stop being a coward and ask me.'

It occurred to me how impossible he could be, a man who would argue every matter, big or small, till the other person was fatally exhausted. Green at the gills. With our differences of temperament, would we ever learn to feel a true sympathy for the way the other's mind worked, the real motives? The train had entered a tunnel and I took refuge in its mighty rumbling (our deafness) to keep from doing as he asked. He seemed to read my thoughts:

'One would have to trust one's instinct some time, don't

you think ... the devil can come up with a million arguments against belief.' We began to laugh. In the next fifteen minutes, Ashwin had spoken to the conductor and moved his bags into my cabin, sentencing the wordless couple immured with us to a night of sleepless outrage.

GLOSSARY

aarti	– worshipping with lamps
ahankar	– pride
amma	– mother
angarakha	– a Rajasthani jacket
arre	– oh
asana	– a cloth mat
babu, babuji	– sir
bajra rotis	– chapattis or unleavened bread made from millet
bandhini	– a form of tie-and-dye printing peculiar to Rajasthan
bandish	– a couplet
baris	– savouries
batua	– a purse
bhairavi	– a raga (musical form – classical)
bhaisaheb	– a brother
bhajan	– a hymn
bhindi	– lady's fingers (okra)
Bhojpuri	– a dialect of Hindi spoken in Bihar and Eastern Uttar Pradesh
bibiji	– local version of marm, mum or ma'am
bindi	– an ornamental mark on the forehead

boudi	– brother's or cousin's wife
bulbul	– bird, term of endearment
carrom	– an indoor game played with round, flat pieces on a large wooden board
chacha	– a paternal uncle
chai	– tea
chalo bhi	– do go on
chameli	– a small white aromatic flower
chatai	– a rush mat
choli	– an ornate local blouse
chooridar-kameez	– a loose knee-length shirt over tight, closely gathered trousers
chowkidar	– a watchman
daal	– lentils
daalmoth	– savoury
Dasshera	– an October festival celebrating the victory of the goddess Durga over the demon Mahishasura, who plagued the world
dhaba	– a roadside café
dhoti	– a single long homespun garment covering the lower limbs
Diwali	– festival of lights around October
Durga	– the mother goddess who fights and conquers demons
firangi	– white foreigner
Ganga and Yamuna	– two sacred rivers meeting at Allahabad
ghagra	– an ornate local skirt
gharana	– a music or dance school
ghazal	– musical composition based on an Urdu poem
ghee	– purified butter
Holi	– spring festival of colours

huzoor	— a master
Id	— a Muslim festival
Id Mubarak ho	— the greetings for the festival of Id
irada	— intention
ittar	— a local perfume
izzat	— self-respect
jalebis	— sweetmeats
janab	— sir
jaunpuri	— name of a raga
jawans	— foot soldiers
jhola	— cloth bag
kaajal	— kohl
kaliyuga	— an age of great evil
kathak	— dance form
Khadakvasla	— a training institute for commissioned officers of the three armed forces
khadder, khadi	— coarse handwoven cotton, popularized by Gandhi
kirtan	— a droning hymn or devotional song
kurta	— knee-length shirt worn over different kinds of pants
Lakshmi	— goddess of wealth
lota	— a mug
Mahadev Shankar	— the god Shiva
mahajan	— a moneylender
mali	— a gardener
mangalsutra	— as necklace with black beads, symbol of wedlock
masala	— spices
mataji	— mother
mausi	— aunt
mulmul	— muslin
paan	— betel leaf
paandaan	— a casket for betel leaf, nuts, etc.

paise	— pice (smallest denomination of Indian currency)
pakoras	— savouries
palla	— a veil
papad	— a poppadom
paratha	— wheat cake roasted lightly in butter
parwal	— a tropical vegetable
pashmina	— woollen shawl with very fine Kashmiri embroidery
pilu	— an evening raga
poories	— deep-fried wheat cakes
Prayag Sangeet Samiti	— a famous music school
raakshas	— a demon
Rabindra sangeet	— songs of Rabindranath Tagore
raga	— a musical form (classical)
Ram kaho!	— Say the name of Ram!
rasgulla, rosogolla	— a white sweet in syrup
Rasoolan Bai	— a singer of exquisite thumris
riaz	— musical practice
Sandilya gotra	— descended from the ancient Brahmin sage Sandilya
sanskaras	— traditions for a caste
sarangi	— a stringed instrument
Saraswati	— the Goddess of learning
Saratchandra	— a Bengali novelist of the early twentieth century, who wrote novels of the deepest idealism and romance
seth	— a rich man, trader
shehnai	— an Indian wind instrument played at concerts and weddings
Shergill, Amrita	— one of India's first modern painters, who lived in the first half of the century and painted mainly groups of women

shlokas	— verses/couplets
Srimati	— Mrs/wife of
taanga	— a horse-drawn cab
taangwala	— the driver of a horse-drawn cab
taanpura	— a stringed instrument
taan	— a very swift succession of notes
takaa	— rupee
takhat	— divan
thali	— brass plate
thakur	— kshatriya, feudal lord
thumri	— a musical form drawing closely on Hindustani classical music
tola	— weight measure
tulsi	— basil
vilambit	— a slow rhythm
vilayat	— England; the Western countries
Vividh Bharati	— radio station relaying Hindi film songs
yaar	— pal
zenana	— women's quarters in a Muslim household